The Deputy Prime Minister

A novel

By Robert Cubitt

By The Same Author
Fiction
The Warriors: The Girl I Left Behind Me (Kindle edition)
The Warriors: Mirror Man (Kindle edition)
The Deputy Prime Minister
The Inconvenience Store

Non-Fiction
I'm So Glad You Asked Me That
Writing A Book That Sells (Kindle edition)
I Want That Job (Kindle edition)

For my wife Bernadette
Who has faith in me.

CHAPTER ONE

The host leant forward a little in his chair before asking his next question.

"Clarke, you have been accused of denigrating one of Britain's great heroes. How do you react to that?"

"The first thing to remember," I replied, realising that the small talk of the introduction was now over, "is that the central character of my book never really existed, or should I say no historical record of his existence can be found. He is a legend, a myth, and as such he can be interpreted in a number of different ways." I paused, allowing the host to interject if he wished to. He didn't. "If he had existed, however, he would have been a man of his time, no more and no less. The legend describes Robin Hood as being an outlaw. My book takes that premise and describes him in terms of the reality of an outlaw of the 12th Century, what he would have been like, how he would have behaved, and how those around him would have behaved. Its all in keeping with the turbulent times that existed then."

"But he is one of the great heroes of British history, how could you describe him as you do, as a murderer and rapist?"

"That is precisely my point, Victor. He doesn't appear in history, he only appears in legend. He is a set of stories handed down by people who needed a hero, a man of the people, to stand up for them. He didn't really exist, so people invented him. If he had existed I think history would have recorded him as being someone very different, which is how I describe him."

"So you don't see Robin Hood as stealing from the rich and giving to the poor."

"Not quite. I have him stealing from anyone who he came across, and its far more profitable to steal from the rich than it is to from the poor. Giving poor people money could be seen as a bribe to persuade them not to betray him to the authorities for the reward money. Not quite so altruistic, I agree, but possibly a more likely motivation for a thief to give away money."

"Many people are up in arms about your book, saying you are anti British, anti heroes. How do you react to that?"

"Lets be clear, my book has a lot of copies so far. It is the media, especially the more right wing newspapers, who are up in arms. The public seems to like my book and the interpretation I place on a period of history."

"OK, but the newspapers suggest that it won't be long before you are portraying Nelson, Wellington, possibly even Churchill as criminals, just to sell books."

"Unlikely, I think. The people you named were real people and history has a lot to say about them. It would be hard for me to portray them in any other way and still keep my books credible." I paused to let my point sink in. "I hope that my readers will always remember that I am telling stories, not recounting history. That I leave to others."

"So, you might think of writing a similar book about another mythical hero, such as, for example, King Arthur."

"Well, I might, if Bernard Cornwall hadn't done such a good job already."

"But Bernard Cornwall didn't have his hero raping women."

"Two separate points there. In his Arthur series Bernard Cornwall leaves all the raping and pillaging to the Saxons. The reality would have been different, with the Celtic warriors doing as much raping of the people they conquered as the Saxons did. In his Sharp series, set around the Peninsular War, he makes it clear that the Redcoats weren't averse to raping the Spanish occupants of cities that they took by storm." I paused to gather my strength for my final sally. "No one accuses Cornwall of being anti-British when he describes the rape of Badajoz."

Victor Maddox conceded the point, then turned to the other guests on the show to bring them into the conversation. I relaxed, satisfied that I had argued my case well, as a minor pop singer admitted that she hadn't even heard of Badajoz, and had no idea where the Peninsular War had been fought, though she thought that Sean Bean was cute. The conversation moved on into a lighter vein, and the last few minutes of the show drifted towards their end.

The Floor Manager shouted "clear" and Victor, myself and the other guests rose and shook hands, prior to leaving the set. The audience filed out and I headed for the make-up room to have the slap removed from my face. I didn't plan on going up to the green room for drinks. No disrespect to either my host or the other guests, I just didn't feel in the mood for sausage rolls and cocktail party chit-chat.

To tell you the truth, television isn't my media. This was my first appearance and might well be my last. Given a free choice I wouldn't have done it, but my publishers said we needed to counter the mauling we were getting in the popular press. My medium is the printed word and always has been, and that is where I believe my future lies.

I had always enjoyed writing, even from an early age. My favourite school lessons had been the ones where we were required to write stories. I never had any trouble writing several pages about what I had done on my holidays. I even wrote stories when I was at home. Rainy afternoons were never a problem for me, as I lost myself in the world of some imaginary character that I had created. I often placed myself as the hero, though that has changed since then.

With my enjoyment of writing it is no surprise to anyone when I studied journalism at University. I had some half formed idea about becoming the next doyen of Fleet Street, but the reality was somewhat different. I never got as far as the local free sheet, let alone Fleet Street.

My first job after Uni was as the assistant editor of a corporate magazine. You know, one of those glossy publications which try to convince the employees that their jobs are important in the great corporate scheme of things. Well, the job title said assistant editor, but as the only other member of staff was the editor herself that title was a little on the grand side. The editor was one of those terribly busy women who is always rushing off to meetings. That left me pretty much to my own devices as far as the magazine was concerned, but the end of the first year I was bored with 'Mary From Accounts Wins £10 on Lottery' type stories.

From there I went into PR as a copywriter. I had never had much time for PR when I was younger, but now I found that PR people weren't the Spawn of Satan as they are often portrayed. They're just ordinary people who try to help other ordinary people look good to their public, whoever their public happens to be. In my case I wrote glossy brochures for sales reps, pamphlets to go inside mail-shots and that sort of thing, for a couple of years, then went up a notch to help out with writing press releases.

In due course the company decided to open a branch in one of the toughest markets in the world: Hollywood. Many small film studios and production companies can't afford to maintain a full time PR department, so as a consultancy that was where we came in. Jolly interesting it was as well. A full campaign would start with a carefully orchestrated rumour that a production was being considered, through to start up press releases, then perhaps a behind the scenes TV production, if the film was going to be particularly spectacular. That was then followed by pre-release publicity, release publicity, and then post release publicity. I went on the TV and radio circuit, baby-sitting the stars as they gave their interviews. I even ended up in the Green Room of Victor Maddox's show on more than one occasion, when I brought the whole circus to Britain.

But the bubble had to burst. We were a small outfit by American standards, and our Branch Manager eventually moved on to pastures new. I waited patiently for the call to tell me I was replacing him, but it never came. Instead I went to work one day to find a stranger sat at the Boss's desk. We discussed my future, and it appeared that I didn't have one. He was going to bring in his own people, so there wasn't any room for me. I could go back to my old job in London, or …..

To say I threw my toys out of the cot would be an understatement. With the benefit of hind sight that probably wasn't a good idea. One never knows when one will need a little good will from an ex-employer. But boy, did it make me feel good.

From there I bummed around for a while. The pay in Hollywood had been generous, and I had little time to spend any of it, so I came back quite comfortably off. At a party one night I spent the whole evening regaling my friends with stories of what Hollywood was really like. As I left one of them said the stories had been really funny, and maybe I should write them down and get them published. Of such chance encounters great empires are built. I did just as had been suggested. The book was a moderate success, certainly making me enough money to bum around for another year.

Then I wrote a novel about how boring bumming around is, and that was moderately successful as well. What had started out as a simple childhood pleasure had turned into gainful employment. *Outlaw*© was my fifth book, and by far my most successful, so far anyway.

I sat in a chair and one of the make-up artists started swabbing my face with cold cream. With my eyes closed I felt, rather than saw, the neighbouring seat being filled. I looked towards the mirror and recognised the face of a well respected political journalist. He smiled towards me as another make-up artist started to apply a dusting of powder to his forehead.

"Good show." He commented. "You made a good point about Robin Hood having been a man of his time, at least if he had ever existed."

"Thanks. Have you read the book?"

"No, not yet. I don't get much time for leisure reading." He added hurriedly "No offence meant."

"None taken. I always feel that the books that I write belong on sunlit beaches, accompanied by something tall and cool."

"Have you anything new under way?" my neighbour asked.

"Not yet. I'm off to the sun to catch up on *my* leisure reading for a couple of weeks, then who knows? I've been thinking of doing something a little more contemporary. Perhaps a thriller."

He fished in his inside pocket and offered something across the gap between our seats.

"My card." He explained. "Give me a ring when you get back. I may have something of interest to you."

The make-up woman had finished her work on him, his healthy tan requiring, as it did , little attention. He rose from his seat, tossed me a quick "Bye for now" and left the room. I examined the small cardboard rectangle as I rose from my own seat. It contained only two bits of information, his name, Steven Rycroft, and a telephone number.

I have to say I was intrigued. Steven Rycroft has a well deserved reputation as a hard hitting journalist, known to ask embarrassing questions of politicians of all parties without fear or favour. What he could have of interest to me I could hardly imagine. I made a mental note, later to be transferred to my diary, to give him a ring on my return from Tenerife. With that I left the studio and returned home to see how my cat had enjoyed my TV appearance.

I live alone in a one bedroom flat in the unfashionable part of Islington. I don't live alone by choice, but I never seemed to have managed to get around to getting married. Well that's not strictly true. There had been a long term relationship, which I had thought might become marriage, when I had lived in LA, but that had ended abruptly when I found out she was seeing at least two other men. Since coming back to the UK I had joined the bachelor circuit, going round from dinner party to dinner party to make up the numbers, and being forced into the company of females who were just as uncomfortable with the situation as I was. What is it about married friends that makes them see it as their bounden duty to play matchmaker at every opportunity?

I must admit that I accepted the invitations without hesitation. As a single thirty-something one's social life is pretty limited if you avoid your married friends, and an evening of small talk with a female stranger is a small price to pay for a home cooked meal. OK, some of the women I was introduced to were attractive and/or witty and intelligent, and under other circumstances I might have asked them out, but I'm afraid that I was determined not to give my friends the satisfaction of thinking they could pick out potential partners for me.

One of the potential partners confided in me that she felt exactly the same way. We stayed in contact for a while, comparing notes and scandal from the various dinner parties we attended, but eventually she found Mr Right, at a friend's dinner party, and so it was goodbye from her.

I was on the publishing circuit now, which got me invites to book launches, gallery openings and those sort of events. At these I had met some very nice women, and had even gone out with a few as a result of those encounters, but as relationships they never seem to go very far.

There was always that 'third date' stage where we would sit looking at each other across a restaurant table, each waiting for the other to say the words that would lead to some sort of longer term commitment. Nothing heavy, you understand. We're not talking about moving in, or marriage, or anything like that, but just making the shift from casual dating to being 'an item'. The words never seemed to come, and so we would part, promising to get in touch soon, but each knowing that the other didn't really mean it. I had to face up to the possibility that I was becoming a full time bachelor. Before long I would be buying a season ticket for the Arsenal and taking up a golf.

The only *significant other* in my life at present was my cat. His name, for some obscure reason, was Alice. I had inherited him from a cousin who had moved abroad, but we had, so far, failed to hit it off. After two years of sharing the same space this was not encouraging. Don't get me wrong, I love cats and usually they love me, especially when I have a tin opener in my hand, but Alice seemed to resent everything about me. My arrival home was usually Alice's signal to disappear through the cat flap, or at least to leave the room. As I arrived home tonight he did both. I don't think he had even watched my television appearance.

Perhaps I shouldn't have called him Alice.

CHAPTER TWO

Holidays are always too brief, and I returned to a chilly London to find the entrance to my small flat blocked with two weeks worth of mail, most of it junk. Hearing me arrive my neighbour, a pleasant if somewhat forgetful elderly lady, carried Alice through the open front door. I tried not to feel hurt as the cat paid more attention to my luggage than it did to me. Lilly and I exchanged a few words about my holiday, with me continually referring to Tenerife and her continually asking about Italy.

Lilly left after a few minutes, still under the impression that I had gone to Italy for my holiday. I put food down for the cat, as I usually did on my return from any trip. Lilly is a wonderful woman, but not having a cat of her own she occasionally forgets when she is looking after mine, and so it is not unusual for Alice to be returned to my keeping with an appetite to rival that of a Sumo wrestler on a diet.

I left the cat tucking into a plate of something brown and smelly, and headed for the tiny alcove I refer to as my office. I switched on the computer and started tackling a fortnight's backlog of e-mails. The majority were from the readers of my latest novel, the one I had been interviewed about by Victor Maddox, which had been forwarded by my publisher. I was pleased to note that the general feeling was that I had painted a realistic picture of the anti-hero, Robin Hood. Only a few were the deranged rantings of right wing bigots who thought Robin Hood was not only a real person, but a great British hero. I triggered of a series of standard replies, in keeping with the view of the original correspondents, and concentrated on the genuine business e-mails that sat in my in-box.

The first was from my agent, reminding me that I had a meeting with her to discuss my new contract with my publishers. On the back of my current book, Outlaw©, she hoped to get me a much better deal. Good news for me. Perhaps I might move out of my shoe box and find something a little more in keeping with being a successful author. Yeah, and pigs might fly I thought, as I remembered the ridiculous price of property inside the circle of the M25.

The second e-mail took me a bit by surprise. It was from Steven Rycroft, repeating his invitation to talk, and suggesting dinner the following week. I typed a quick note of acceptance, anxious not to let the opportunity slip away. Curiouser and curiouser, I thought, totally without originality. The good Steven obviously had something eating at him.

Once people find out that you are an author they often tell you what a wonderful idea they have for a story. They are usually wrong, and I don't encourage people like that. Steven Rycroft, however, was different. Firstly he is a published author in his own right. OK, he writes non-fiction, but that doesn't change the basic fact. Secondly, Rycroft will know many writers because he works in television, where everyone is a writer, or thinks they are. If he was pursuing me then he must have a good reason, or at least my natural arrogance allowed me to think so.

I quickly worked through the remaining e-mails, and then shut down my computer. I was tired after my flight, as well as hungry. I put Steven Rycroft out of my mind and settled back into my normal domestic routine. My cat continued to ignore me and went off to sleep in the centre of my bed.

*   *   *

I arrived at Steven Rycroft's front door at the appointed time. It was a pleasant enough looking terraced house in Fulham, which had stayed very fashionable with media types despite the Jill Dando murder. The door was opened by an attractive woman, who introduced herself as Valerie, Steven's PA. I tried to suppress thoughts about possible alternative meanings for the initials "PA". Well, she was very attractive.

A man would have to be made of stone to find Valerie anything other than attractive. She was quite tall, probably near to 6 feet in height. She had elegant curves, which were obvious even though she tried to keep them modestly hidden beneath a severe business suit. Her face was squarish, her cheeks descending from high cheek bones to a slightly pointed chin. Her eyes were a deep brown, competing with the deep chestnut colour of her short cut hair. She could have walked down any cat walk in Europe had she chosen to, and graced the cover of many a magazine. That she was working for Steven Rycroft I considered to be very opportune. I hoped to get to know Valerie a lot better.

Valerie offered me a glass of wine, telling me that Steven was in the kitchen preparing dinner, and would be out in a moment. She disappeared upstairs, returning a few minutes later wearing a coat. She called towards the back of the house, telling Steven that "she'd be off now then." A muffled shout was returned, as Valerie closed the front door behind her.

I surveyed the room, trying to divine who the off screen Steven Rycroft might be. The room was plainly if comfortably furnished. A few tasteful if inexpensive prints adorned the walls, but the overall impression of the room was of comfortable utility. "Pied a Terre" I concluded. A Monday to Friday residence. Steven's real home, I guessed, was somewhere else. Pictures of a "little woman" making jam in a country cottage sprang to mind, along with pictures of Valerie wearing something sheer and slinky as she typed Steven's e-mails in Steven's London house.

I heard a sound behind me and turned to see Steven entering the room, a glass of white wine in his hand, which he offered to me. I rose to greet him, shaking his hand. His grip was firm, but never threatened to injure. Steven is quite a large man, and such people are occasionally inclined to forget their own strength.

"Dinner will be ready in a few minutes." Steven advised me, as he waved me back into my chair.

"Will your wife be joining us?" I fished.

"No, not today." He didn't elaborate, and so I decided to let the matter lie. Steven asked me about my holiday, and we spent the few minutes before dinner discussing the delights of the Canary Islands.

I knew a little about Steven Rycroft. I had done some cursory research, trying to discover something to tell me what this meeting might be about. Steven had finished his education at Stowe School, and then gone on to University at Oxford. From there he had taken a job in the newsroom of a regional TV station, rising through the organisation until he had ended up working for a national news network as a political correspondent. When a fledgling broadcaster had started up in the South East, Steven Rycroft had been a natural choice to front its current affairs programming. He was now a regular face on both regional and national television, and first choice to conduct the harder hitting interviews.

At last Steven ushered me through to the back of the house, which was taken up by a large and very pleasant kitchen/dining area. The table was already laid out, with plates of paté and salad occupying the two place settings.

"Cooking is my secret passion." Steven confided. "Had I not studied politics at University I probably would have become a chef. That would have *pleased* my father." The emphasis he placed on the word "pleased" suggested it would have had the opposite affect.

"Would your father not have approved?"

"Dad was a career soldier." Steven answered. "What he wanted from all his sons was the same commitment to public service, and if that also included the Army, then so much the better. I fear he is sadly disappointed. My elder brother is a management consultant, my younger is a catholic priest. And I'm the lowest of the low, because I'm a journalist, and a TV one to boot. The only saving grace, as far as he is concerned, is that I talk to politicians. If I were to cook their dinners I would be beyond the pale as far as he was concerned."

As we finished the excellent paté we discussed careers and father's expectations. My wine glass seemed to refill itself, though I don't recall Steven touching the bottle that sat in the wine cooler.

A roast duck, served with crispy vegetables and a delicious sauce, followed the pate. Steven would have made a fortune had he followed his instincts and become a chef. He had a real talent. The small talk continued relentlessly. No matter how I tried to turn Steven to the reason for my visit he always managed to fend me off.

As this was a male only dinner, Steven explained, he had dispensed with a pudding, and gone for cheese instead. An aromatic selection of cheeses was accompanied by an excellent vintage Port. Leaving the debris of the dinner table we carried the Port bottle back into the lounge, where the level dropped steadily for the next hour or so.

Steven at last came to the reason for my visit.

"Have you ever heard of Timothy Elgin?"

"Of course, Deputy Prime Minister, darling of the party, Prime Minister-in-waiting." Of all things I had expected, I hadn't expected to be asked a foolish question.

"Correct. And incorrect." Steven gazed deep into his Port, as though looking for the right words to say next. At last he found them. "He's all the things you said. But he is a whole lot more. He is a thief, a cheat, a liar, and probably the most corrupt politician so far this century, possibly the most corrupt since the 17th century. He may even be responsible for a murder."

This was all news to me, as it would be to most of the British electorate. Everywhere Elgin went he was lionised. It was universally agreed that he was the only credible successor to the current Prime Minister, and it was only a matter of when, not if, he took on the mantle of Government. I started to say as much, but Steven raised his hand to still my protest.

"Of course, no one knows about the other Timothy Elgin, but I have been studying him for some time now, and I have a huge mass of information about him that very few people even suspect exists. He has taken bribes, he has used his political influence to protect criminals, he has corrupted others on his own account. In short he is a thoroughly nasty piece of work."

"So why not expose him? You have all the contacts necessary to put together a block buster exposé that any TV company would kill for."

"You missed a key word in what I said." responded Steven, gently. "I said I have *information*. It isn't the same as evidence. If I repeated one word of what I just said in public I would be sued left, right and centre. And Elgin would win the case, have no doubt about that."

"So find the evidence then." I suggested, in my naiveté.

"The people who have the evidence are the least likely to stand up in court and testify. Remember the Archer case? It took a falling out with a co-conspirator to convict Archer. Elgin isn't so careless."

"OK, but the obvious question is 'why tell me?'". I was getting a little impatient, wanting Steven to get to the point.

"I can't present a case as fact, as I said, but I could, or rather you could, present it as fiction. Write the whole shoddy business up as a novel, but get as close as you can to real life. Maybe some people can be frightened into coming forward as witnesses to give evidence. It would only take a few well presented newspaper articles and Elgin would have to either sue or resign. Either way it would probably be enough to trigger a police investigation into his activities." He lay back in his chair, waiting for my reaction.

I took a few moments to think over what he had said. It made sense. Without witnesses it would be hopeless, and very expensive, to go public with Steven's allegations. Even rumours in the press might be enough to warrant an injunction. I was happy enough to write a political novel, but the idea of being sued for everything I had wasn't very welcoming. Mind you, Elgin was welcome to the cat.

"I can see how that would work, but surely it's a second best option. Why not use investigative journalists to put a case together that would hold enough water for it to be published. Its been done before."

"It has, and its also failed before. Remember Archer again. The papers thought they'd done enough to make sure they would win a libel case, if they were sued. They lost because the legal establishment believed Archer before it would believe them. Without any credible witnesses no paper will risk having to pay the sort of damages that are awarded these days. The shareholders don't like it. Don't think I haven't explored this route already. I've sounded out a couple of editors, hypothetically. They dismissed it out of hand."

"OK, let's say I agree, how does it work?"

"Valerie and I have been researching Elgin for two years now, off and on, mainly Valerie as I have my TV journalism to keep me occupied. We turn all that research over to you, and you do your own research to see what you can come up with to confirm, or deny, what we already have. We continue to monitor Elgin, using our own resources, and keep you up to date with everything we get on him. If we can get hard evidence we will go public anyway, but you will still have a cracking good novel, which should sell even better if people think its based on real life."

It made sense. Robert Harris pulled off a similar trick with his book "Ghost". Either way I come out a winner. That immediately made me suspicious.

"What's in it for you?" the cynic in me asked.

"Well, I do expect a co-author credit, and one for Valerie, and a share of the earnings. Shall we say 40% of the gross."

"Shall we say 40% of the net? And you share with Valerie" I retaliated. My agent would probably murder me in my sleep for that. "But there must be more to it than just a share of the income. If the book doesn't sell you would make hardly anything, whether its gross or net."

"My real motivation is to get Elgin. He belittles politics simply by being where he is. If he became Prime Minster who knows what damage he might do. We have always been very lucky in this country. We may throw up the odd dodgy MP or councillor from time to time, but its usually either small time stuff or they're all in it together, like the expenses scandal. If he ever got the top job this country could start looking like a banana republic in no time flat." He paused, to allow himself time to recover his composure.

"OK, it all sounds very idealistic, but Elgin has done some real damage to some people who weren't able to protect themselves. Politicians should be protecting people like that, not doing the hurting. He belongs in prison, and I want to be the one who puts him there."

A vision flitted across my mind of Steven Rycroft accepting a Pulitzer prize, and that was enough to convince me of his motives. Of one thing I had no doubt, Rycroft was a journalist to his core.

"So why not write the book yourself? Why share with me?

"Two reasons, first the time it would take. My schedule is jammed solid for the next 3 years almost, and it would be too risky to pull out of my commitments. If it all went wrong I would have made some powerful enemies in the business, some of whom might also be implicated in Elgin's crimes. Secondly I write non-fiction. Its dull, boring, and intended for students to pour over in the dead of night as they study for exams. You, on the other hand, can bring a plot to life and create characterisations and dialogue that I could only ever dream of

I had read a couple of Rycroft's books and he was being far too modest, but I could see his point. "Have you approached anyone else with this idea?"

"No, it only occurred to me the night we met at the studios. To tell you the truth, I hadn't thought out how to get the story into the public domain. I've only really thought it through over the last couple of weeks, while you were on holiday."

"OK, I think we have a deal. I'll let my agent know and she can get the relevant papers drawn up. What happens next?"

"I'll put Valerie at your disposal until further notice. What she normally does for me she can put in the hands of a temp. She'll contact you, and we'll get together soon and talk over the broad strategy. I'll leave tactics to you and Valerie."

"Just one more thing. What if Elgin gets wind of this?"

"Oh, Clarke, I'm counting on him getting wind of it. I want him worried. I want him scared. Because if he's scared and worried he might make a mistake, and then we'll have him."

We finished off the Port (well it seemed a shame not to) and I bade him farewell. The thought of spending time with Valerie was a pleasing one, which I let slip. I tried to recover the situation, making it clear I didn't want to tread on anyone's toes. He laughed, and stepped over to small desk.

"I usually put this away when entertaining someone for the first time. I don't like my home life becoming too public." Out of a drawer Steven took a photograph frame, which he handed to me. I looked into the photograph and was met by the fine boned, sensitive face of a well known concert pianist. Even a Philistine such as myself recognised that face. "That's Gustav, my *wife* as you might say. We share a cottage in Oxfordshire, though he's on a world tour at present." OK. So I was half right. "I'd appreciate your discretion. As I said, I like my private life to remain private, and my relationship with Gustav is nobody's business but ours."

I assured Steven that his secret was safe with me.

Smiling Steven showed me to the door, my taxi standing waiting for me in the street outside. Steven said goodnight, and I tottered across the pavement and fell into the rear seat of the cab. On my return home my cat continued to ignore me.

CHAPTER THREE

The thing about being a writer that I like the best is research. To bury oneself in archives, libraries and the internet for weeks on end allows one to escape from the reality of life. So it was with a light heart that I launched myself into researching Timothy Elgin. I started with the *files*, as they are called, of the daily newspapers, most of which are now accessible on line.

There followed two days of enjoyable browsing, my 'phone unplugged and my doorbell unanswered. The files took me back to the time when Elgin was first elected to Parliament, with a couple of minor articles on his record in local Government. His rise to prominence had been truly amazing. Seen over his nine years at Westminster it probably looks nothing outstanding, but seen in one continuous story it becomes apparent that he was a very favoured individual. To get back further than nine years I would have to visit the local newspapers that covered the area where he lived. These, sadly, are as yet unavailable on-line.

I took the train to Wroxborough, the industrial town in the Midlands that Timothy Elgin had once called home. Fortunately it was also the home to both the County newspaper and the small local weekly owned by the same company. A disinterested receptionist showed me into a cubby hole fitted out with a micro-fiche and printer. My cover story about researching a biography attracted no more interest than if I had announced that I had come to refill the vending machines.

Elgin had obviously been a prominent and active local politician. Hardly a week went by when one of the two newspapers hadn't run an article that mentioned his name. He was photographed with businessmen and women, charity workers, minor royalty, cutting ribbons, planting trees and unveiling plaques, as well as at a host of receptions and dinners. His name appeared regularly as a speaker in the Council Chamber at County Hall. Each name he was linked to then became another lead that had to be run down and checked out for dubious activities. How I would manage such a wealth of information I had yet to work out, but perhaps Steven Rycroft's own files might help to narrow down the search. As Elgin had been a County Councillor it also meant that I had to check out other newspapers in the county, and so it was three days before I was able to return to my flat in London.

I returned to be ignored once again by my cat, and to be greeted by my agent, Dana Smith, who had been let into my flat by the ever obliging Lilly. There followed a *full and frank exchange of views*, which others might call a blazing row. Firstly I had upset her by missing the appointment we had scheduled the previous week, and not returning her calls or answering my door bell when she called round. "You could have been dead for all I know" She screamed, "Or is that just wishful thinking?" Then she was mad because of the deal I had agreed to with Steven Rycroft. This particularly upset her, because she was sure she could have got

Rycroft down to 20%, and had him funding most of my research activity.

It took an enormous and expensive lunch to calm Dana down. She left the restaurant grumbling, but at least she was now down to the level of a mildly active volcano, rather than in full, lava spitting flow.

I returned home to address my e-mail backlog, and found an invitation to meet Steven for our strategy meeting.

*   *   *

Steven's office is the converted front bedroom of his house, which he had turned into a light, airy and thoroughly pleasant working environment. It was such a contrast to my own dingy work place that I couldn't help feeling jealous. Against two walls stood modern desks, one for him and one for Valerie apparently, each fronted by comfortable swivel chairs. A third wall was lined by filing cabinets and book shelves that sagged under the weight of their contents. The final space was the bay of the front window, which was filled by a large, well stuffed sofa. I settled myself into this as Steven and Valerie swivelled their chairs round to face the room. The final item of any note in the room was an easel, mounted on which was a cork backed bulletin board. Pinned to this were a handful of photos', the significance of which Steven started to explain to me.

At the top in the centre was the unmistakable face of the Deputy Prime Minister, Timothy Elgin. Below that was the photo of a good looking blond man of about the same age.

"Otto Langsdorf." Stated Steven. "Chief Executive and majority shareholder of Langsdorf Developments, a major Midlands property development company. We believe that he slipped Elgin backhanders to make sure that various planning applications went through without too much difficulty. Elgin and Langsdorf have known each other for years, which is no secret."

"Hold on a mo." I objected. "Elgin has never had anything to do with Planning. Firstly he was a County Councillor, which is the second tier of planning authority, not the primary decision maker, and secondly he didn't serve on the County Planning Committee either."

"Both true statements." Responded Steven. "That doesn't mean that he didn't exert influence though, or act as a go-between. These are the two Prime Suspects." He tapped the pictures on either side of Langsdorf's. One was of a middle aged, rather plain woman, and the other was of a nondescript looking man, also in middle age. "Daphne Gibson and David Trace. Gibson was Chair of the Planning Committee for Wroxborough District Council, and Trace was the same for Nethertop District Council. Gibson never held paid employment in her life, and her husband was a milkman. They lived in a Council house until five years ago, but now live in a villa on the Algarve that is valued, at a conservative estimate, at a half a million pounds. Trace still lives locally, but well beyond his means."

"OK, so they may both have been taking backhanders, but that doesn't implicate Elgin." I had to pick holes in the arguments, to find out how robust they were. If I couldn't be convinced that something dodgy was going on then there was no way I could convince the reading public.

"You're quite right." Conceded Steven. "But we have a lot of anecdotal evidence that Langsdorf was working through Elgin, and that he either bribed the councillors himself, or exerted influence in some way. I would guess its a bit of both. Then there are the appeals. Several of the planning applications went to appeal, which the County Council arbitrated on. Elgin, as Leader of the Council, appointed the councillors that sat on the appeals panels. That would give him direct influence over the decision making process which, on all occasions, went in favour of Langsdorf."

"That's fair enough," I conceded. "But it still doesn't mean he bribed District Councillors, though. I'll need more than that." I paused and gathered my thoughts. "The idea here is for me to paint a picture that will frighten witnesses into coming into the open, and which will encourage journalists to conduct their own investigations. We might even want to suggest that the Police start investigating Elgin. That means that everything I write has to be based on the truth. If I start creating fantasies around the connections between Elgin and other people the journo's will spot them very quickly and abandon their searches because they'll believe the whole book is fiction, instead of thinly disguised fact."

"This is going to be harder than we thought." Chipped in Valerie. Up to now she had been silent, taking notes on our conversation. I was intrigued by her use of the term *we*. I had understood that the project was Rycroft's, but this suggested a more direct involvement by Valerie herself. I filed this way for future analysis.

"Yes," agreed Steven. "We're going to have to get more information than we currently have if we're going to give Clarke what he needs. No matter, for the moment. Lets get on." That use of the word *we* again, I noted.

"As well as being a property development company, Langsdorf Development also owns several smaller companies, some of which specialise in building maintenance." Steven continued his case against Elgin. "At the time when Elgin was first elected to the County Council they didn't hold any local government maintenance contracts. By the time he left they held several District Council contracts and a couple of County Council ones. The problem is that they won the contracts with bids that were considerably higher than expected. Again we have anecdotal evidence of skullduggery. The holders of the contracts when they went for re-tender either decided not to tender, or withdrew their tenders. So did other likely competitors. So Langsdorf's companies won the contracts by default."

"I haven't heard anything to suggest any wrong doing." I interjected.

"The anecdotes we have suggest that intimidation was used, and in at least one case direct violence, to persuade competitors to withdraw their bids, or not to bid for the contracts in the first place. The interesting thing is that this was only done against the companies that were likely to submit low bids. High bidders were left alone as they weren't considered to be a threat." Steven paused to let this information sink in. "The tendering process is confidential, so someone on the inside had to be leaking information on the bids, so that Langsdorf, or someone acting on his behalf, knew which companies to target."

"That could be any junior clerk in the council. Nothing there to link this to Elgin."

"One junior clerk in one council, yes they could be bribed, possibly even two clerks in different councils. But five clerks in five councils? I think not. Elgin, on the other hand, could ask for the tendering information from all the councils on some official pretext, and then leak it. That's a much more likely scenario, and remember, we've already established his link to Langsdorf."

"Fair enough, but we're going to need some sort of proof that it happened. We can't just make it an unfounded allegation, even in a work of fiction. The dog just won't run unless its got all four legs."

"I think this is going to be a recurring theme." Valerie commented. "Can we assume that we have to support all of these allegations in a more substantial way? You just give me examples of the sorts of things you need, and we'll see what we can do." *We* again.

"Dates, times, places, people who saw, or heard, something that we can use." I replied. "I'll change their names in the book, obviously, but those people need to be able to recognise themselves, and they're the ones we want to flush out into the open. And when the journo's come sniffing around we can drop a few hints as to which rocks they should be looking under."

Valerie made a note on her pad, while Steven went on with building his case.

"Everything we have so far is in here." He indicated a thick grey box file. He opened it up and took out a single sheet of paper, which he passed over to me. "These are companies that have benefited from Government decisions. Unlike previous administrations there is no smoking gun evidence of donations to party funds, peerages or anything like that. There are no leaked e-mails or copies of memos, either. However, Elgin has contacts with all of these companies in one way or another. You'll find newspaper articles with pictures of him and various people from these companies." This I could check for myself from my trawl through the archives.

"What sort of benefits are we talking about here? "I asked.

"A few examples, then. just to whet your appetite. Craven Armaments won a contract to supply small arms to the Republic of Voltava, right after the Government announced that it would provide military equipment to help defend the Republic against its more aggressive neighbours. National Hydro won the contract to build a dam in Asia right after the Overseas Development Agency announced that it would be providing funding for the project. Our old friends Langsdorf Developments bought up a whole lot of surplus Ministry of Defence land at knock down prices, then got planning permission almost on the nod, despite some of the land being protected habitat. Need I go on? Its all in the file." He tapped the lid of the box.

I agreed that there were some interesting coincidences, a phrase that made Steven smile. "Interesting indeed" he grinned.

"I'd like to meet Elgin. Can it be arranged?"

"For what purpose?" asked Steven.

"In order to create a convincing picture of him I need to get behind the newspaper articles to find out about the real man. I need to be able to understand his psyche in order to convince the readers, and particularly the journo's, that the man I'm writing about is Elgin, and not some fictional creation."

"Good point." Steven conceded. "Any thoughts about how we could engineer a meeting?" The question was directed to both me and to Valerie.

"How about faking an interview for TV?" suggested Valerie. "If we persuade Elgin that Metro TV is going to do a profile on him, then we can send Clarke along posing as a researcher doing *background* on him."

"His ego is big enough to go for that." Agreed Steven. "I'm not sure we should involve Metro though. Its very close to home."

"It'll be OK so long as he doesn't check back with them, and why should he? By the time he discovers its a fake it will be too late. If he starts asking questions early on we can backtrack, say that the editor has reconsidered and decided against doing a profile at this time. It's a common enough occurrence." Persuaded Valerie.

"Just make sure Elgin can't trace it back to us." Commanded Steven. "I don't want to end up in front of the Broadcasting Standards Commission.

We tidied up a few loose ands, and Valerie agreed to try to set up the interview. I went home, the grey box file tucked under my arm. My cat scratched me when I tried to pet it.

CHAPTER FOUR

I ploughed my way through the box file of "evidence" to see what sort of sense I could make of it. Much of it consisted of hand written notes recording little bits of information that people had let slip about Elgin's relationships with Langdorf and others. I soon came to recognise Valerie's neat script and Steven's more flamboyant hand, but there was a third lot of handwriting which I couldn't yet identify. I used one wall of my tiny office to sketch out the links I could establish. One stood out quite clearly, and hadn't been mentioned before.

Elsa Peters was Elgin's election agent. Since he had become an MP this had become a full-time job for her, but in his days on the County Council she had done the same job for a number of other local politicians. It didn't take long to establish that Elsa had been election agent for both Daphne Gibson and David Trace. OK, it wasn't much, but it did establish a clear link from Elgin to the two suspect Chairs of Planning Committees.

There was no doubt that Elgin was a common factor in of some very lucrative business activities that had resulted from governmental decisions. However, it took only a short time on the internet to establish that several other politicians from both sides of the House had very similar connections. So if the evidence applied to Elgin then it also applied to those others.

I began to summarise Elgin's political career, to try to help with some of the chronology.

Elgin had been quite a distinguished scholar, firstly at his local Grammer School and then later at Oxford University, where he studied politics and economics, coming away with a double first. Having been active in the political life of the University it came as no surprise when he won a prized post as a researcher for an MP in his favoured party. The fact that the party was in opposition didn't disturb him. This seems to be the point at which he first came into contact with Otto Langsdorf. Despite his Germanic name, Langsdorf was born and bred in the same town as Elgin himself. Langsdorf was a struggling entrepreneur who was constantly lobbying his MP for political support for his own business activities.

Local party influence provided Elgin with a safe ward when he decided to enter politics as a full time local government politician. Family money meant that, ostensibly, Elgin was able to support himself without needing to work. I made a mental note to find out just how much family money had been available. The source of the money appeared to stem from a newly acquired bride, the daughter of a prominent party supporter. Camilla Elgin appeared regularly on the arm of her husband, and the arrival of children, two girls, in quick succession, completed the picture of a happy family.

Elgin rose rapidly through the party hierarchy in the County Council, and when control of the council changed hands after a particularly hard fought election, Elgin was elected its leader as a result of a unanimous vote by his own party's councillors. Here I started to find the first links between Elgin and some of the companies that were later to benefit from Government decisions. Many had branches or factories within the county, and Elgin, in his official capacity as Leader of the Council and patron of various local charities, was invited to many sporting and charitable events. I had no doubt that these would all have been registered as *interests* so that Elgin could not be accused of being covert about these links, though this is something else I would have to check out.

In my own pile of clippings I found a photo of Elgin presenting a golfing trophy to the Chairman of Craven Armaments, and then a picture of Elgin and a number of other people seated around a banqueting table in the company of the Marketing Director of National Hydro. And so it went on.

After one term of office as Leader of the Council a snap General Election was called, and Elgin stood down from his position on the council, to be immediately selected to stand as MP for his local constituency. If he was opposed for his candidacy there was no record of it. As a safe seat he was elected with a suitably large majority. So began the rise up the greasy pole of Westminster politics. For Elgin the rise was rapid. From the back benches he became a junior whip within six months, then a Junior Minister responsible, not surprisingly, for local Government. After a reshuffle caused by his principle being found by a journalist in a compromising position with a prostitute, Elgin took over the top job. Another General Election came and went, and Elgin found himself firstly in charge of the Home Office, and then Deputy Prime Minister. I made a note to check out the story of the Minister and the prostitute. It sounded very convenient, which had not gone unnoticed at the time, though Elgin's name hadn't been linked to the demise of the Minister.

Under previous administrations the post of Deputy Prime Minister had been a meaningless title, used to salve the ego of senior politicians who were on their way out of high office. Under the present Prime Minister, however, this had changed. The post now meant that the incumbent was a favoured person being groomed for the most senior office in the country. The role required the incumbent to make political statements on a range of issues, allowing the relevant ministers to be seen to take more statesman like roles. Elgin was at the heart of major decision making, and exerted considerable political influence over his leader.

Again the newspapers provided a fund of stories about this prominent politician, touring factories, making speeches to conferences, writing columns for friendly newspapers explaining Government Policy, Elgin was clearly no shrinking violet. But nowhere could I find even the tiniest hint that he was anything less than a perfect public servant. My wall now resembled a spider's web, but at the centre of it the spider wasn't Elgin, it was his agent, Elsa Peters.

I rang Steven's number, and Valerie answered the 'phone.

"Yes, we're aware of Elsa Peter's relationship with Elgin," Valerie's replied in answer to what I told her, "but we hadn't connected her to Gibson and Trace. Well done you."

"Any progress with the interview?" I asked.

"I was just about to ring you about that. Next Tuesday, in Elgin's constituency office in Wroxborough. I suggest we go up the night before. It'll give us a chance to work out an interview plan."

"We?" I queried.

"Oh yes. You're the Producer of the programme that is going to profile Elgin, and I'm your PA. Hope you don't mind."

It wouldn't have mattered if I had. I was faced with a fait accompli.

"Why Wroxborough? Why not his Westminster office?"

"He's claiming to be up there on constituency business, but that's a lie. I rang the constituency party chairman, and he told me there are no meetings planned, and any way, if they need Elgin present for anything they arrange the meeting for the weekends when he's up there to hold surgeries anyway."

"Well, he is the MP and we're just the peasants, so I guess we have to go where he wants us." I commented.

"Yes, but it is typical of the arrogance of the man to drag us halfway across the country. But as you say, if we want to talk to him we have to go where he wants us to. It might not be to his advantage though." I wondered what Valerie meant by that, but she didn't seem keen to elaborate.

We quickly agreed an itinerary. "Oh, have you got a track-suit, a dark one?" Valerie asked, somewhat surprisingly. My mind floated to the sweaty heap on the floor of my wardrobe, which had been there since my last abortive attempt to get fit. I told her that I had. "Pack it, and a pair of trainers." she instructed, before saying good bye and hanging up the 'phone. I stayed my curiosity, difficult as it was.

The prospect of spending a night in a hotel with Valerie was a welcome one. OK, we would be in separate rooms, but we would still spend quite a lot of the time together. Then there was the train ride up there as well. As a Londoner I never saw the need to own a car. With four wheeled progress through the city being at a snail's pace I found that the underground served my purposes more than adequately. If I did need a car for my occasional sorties into rural Britain I hired one. But I liked the train. OK, they often run late, and some of the suburban services bear more resemblance to a rubbish tip than a form of transport, but there is something relaxing about speeding through the country side at 100 mph, without having to worry about traffic police or other drivers. There is also the advantage that one can work on a train, which one can't do in a car, at least not if one wishes to live a long time.

I wondered if Valerie found me as attractive as I found her. So far she had given me no signs either way. When we had met last time she had been extremely business like in her approach, and I had the feeling that she wouldn't mix business with pleasure. She wasn't unfriendly though. Her smile when she greeted me was warm enough, but I had learnt through experience not to read too much into that.

I returned to my research. Every avenue gradually closed down. Elgin's family money came in the form of a legacy from his father in law, plus a small inheritance from his own parents. It accounted for him not needing to work while he had been a councillor. Once in Parliament he had lived on his income, or so it would seem. His apartment in London was rented at a commercial rate, and one could assume that his house in Wroxbourough was mortgaged. That made for some expensive outgoings. In the Register of Members' Interests Elgin declared quite a lot of income from a small PR company that he owned, but there was nothing to suggest that he was actively involved in running the business, or that he might be exerting influence as a result of this business relationship.

It did occur to me that the PR Company, called Get Real Communications, would be a useful way of laundering money earned by illicit means, but without access to the accounts there would be no way of proving it. Certainly the Company's House records suggested that this was a highly successful business, but my old colleagues in PR had never heard of Get Real Communications. Inconclusive, perhaps, but it did suggest to me that Steven Rycroft was on to something significant.

I rang Rycroft with this news.

"We were wondering about Get Real." Acknowledged Steven. "We rang them on the pretext of wanting to hire them for a job for Metro TV, but they weren't interested. They said they had a full order book. Most unusual. Have you ever heard of a consultancy turning down work?"

I admitted that I hadn't. "Who did you speak to?"

"A woman called Tracy Purvis. I haven't come across the name anywhere else, though. I have to say that I don't think Tracy runs the show. Something about the way she dealt with me suggested that she isn't a PR professional. I got the impression she's just there to answer the 'phones."

I thanked Steven for this tit-bit of information. The Company's House website provided me with the address of the Registered Office for Get Real Communications. The location was London E9, which turned out to be Hackney. From my address there was no easy route by underground, so I took a taxi. The address turned out to be the offices of a solicitor, who displayed a series of brass plaques that announced that premises to be the registered office of about 20 different businesses.

I haven't that much experience dealing with solicitors, but one thing I do know is that they don't talk about their client's business. This was confirmed to me when I entered the small and rather scruffy reception area. A bleached blonde woman put up an impenetrable wall when I asked about one of the companies that was registered there. I deliberately avoided mentioning Get Real Communications, but I don't think it would have made any difference if I had used their name. If this platinum harridan wasn't going to tell me about Axial Electronics Ltd it was unlikely that she would be any more forthcoming about any of the other clients.

I took another taxi back home again, feeling thoroughly deflated. I don't know why I should have felt this way. It was early days yet, and I shouldn't expect all my questions to be answered, but for some reason I felt thwarted. Here I had a reasonable lead that should have taken me closer to finding out about Timothy Elgin, and all I had achieved was a wasted taxi ride. A thought crossed my mind that I might break into the solicitor's office and raid the files, but I dismissed it almost as soon as it popped into my head. Firstly I wasn't burglar, and would probably leave so much evidence behind me that I might as well hand myself into the nearest police station. The second was that there might not be any records held at those offices at all. The fact that they were the registered office of the company didn't mean they did any more than forward mail for the companies that they represented.

My cat gave me one of those looks that only a cat can give. Its half way between a sneer and a jeer. When I shut myself away in my cubby hole of an office I'm sure I heard him laugh.

CHAPTER FIVE

The following Monday afternoon found myself and Valerie on the train heading North. If Valerie felt the same way about spending a night in a hotel with me then she kept her feelings to herself.

Forced into spending some free time with me she opened up a little bit, and told me something about herself. I had a feeling she wasn't telling me everything, an instinct that proved to be correct, but at least she lowered her guard enough for me to find out something about the woman behind the business suit.

Valerie had grown up in Nottingham with her mother, an aunt and an uncle. She also had a brother apparently, but didn't speak about him much. She went to the local school, and then to a technical college where she learned to be a secretary. After a series of dead end jobs in Nottingham she decided to try her hand in the big city and headed South to London. She had been fortunate to get her current position with Steven Rycroft almost as soon as she arrived. Valerie admitted that she would never get rich out of this job, but she was paid enough to allow her to rent a bedsit in Camden and to run a small car. The collaboration on this book, she hoped, would help her to pay off her credit card bills and the HP on her car, at the very least. I tried not to build up her hopes on that score. The publishing game can be very unpredictable, as the book reading public can be very fickle.

Valerie didn't talk a great deal about her private life, but I was relieved when she confessed that she didn't currently have a boyfriend. She knew few people in London, and didn't go out much by herself. She often acted as escort (in the true meaning of the word) to Steven Rycroft when he needed someone on his arm at dinner parties and gala events, and she enjoyed those. If people assumed that she and Rycroft were in a relationship then it suited them both.

Valerie had met some nice people while moving in that circle and was starting to establish a social life, but it was slow going. I sympathised with her, and found that she was also a victim of the match making married friends. We laughed about the efforts of these well meaning people. I shared my thoughts about taking up a hobby, and Valerie laughed at this. She confided that she had also been thinking along those lines, but more in terms of taking up evening classes. We giggled about the potential entertainment value of pottery or flower arranging for improving our social lives. It was good to hear Valerie laugh. I made a more serious suggestion, that she study creative writing. She played down her abilities, but I felt that deep down she might have some creative talent.

All too soon our journey ended, and Valerie became business like once again, organising a taxi to the hotel and dealing with the receptionist, just as an efficient PA would.

We were booked into one of those corporate hotels that seem to exist in order to destroy the idea that staying in hotels is a pleasant experience. We took the precaution of finding a local restaurant in which to eat dinner, both of us knowing that the hotel dining room would not meet our needs. Over dinner we planned out the interview structure, with me telling Valerie the sort of things I wanted to know about Elgin, and Valerie framing questions that would fit into the sort of programme format that we were supposed to be producing.

"Why have I been promoted to Producer? I haven't the foggiest what a producer does. Is it just so that you could come along?"

"Not at all." Valerie denied, though I still had my suspicions. "We realised after you left last week that you were really too old to be a researcher, they're all 20 somethings straight out of University. We had to find something that fitted your age a little better, and Producer seemed to fit the bill. I had to come along because no producer would ever take their own notes or carry their own brief case, so you needed a PA, and who better for that role than me?"

It all made perfect sense, though later it would all seem so contrived, but we weren't at *later* then. We finished our meal, which was quite an acceptable standard considering we were in the provinces, and walked the short distance back to the hotel. Valerie pleaded work commitments and went straight to her room, while I went through to the bar for a drink. I only stayed for one, as I felt that my presence in the bar would crowd the only other person in there - the barman. I too retired to my room.

I was watching highlights of a football match on satellite TV when my mobile 'phone rang.

"Did you bring that tracksuit?" Valerie's voice asked. I said that I had. "Put it on, make sure you have something warm underneath, and meet me in the car park in five minutes." I was about to ask a whole raft of questions, but the line went dead. I did as I was told. It was the only way I was going to get my questions answered.

In the car park I found Valerie standing beside a hatchback car, keys in one hand and a small rucksack in the other. "Hire car" she explained, forestalling the need for me to ask where the car had come from. "I arranged for it to be delivered." I got into the passenger seat, while Valerie climbed in on the driver's side and we set off. Naturally I asked her where we were going. She told me that the less I knew the better, but all would be revealed if her plan worked out.

We drove out along one of the main roads for a couple of miles, then turned off into a suburb. I couldn't see what sort of area we were in, but the long walls interrupted by the occasional gate suggested private housing. Very private housing. From the ease with which Valerie identified turnings it was obvious that she had been there before. At last we stopped and got out of the car. Valerie slung her rucksack onto her back, and told me to jog along side her. Remembering the last time I had jogged anywhere I hoped that we weren't going too far. My prayers were answered. We turned off one street and onto another when Valerie stopped jogging. Looking carefully around her she pulled me close to a wall and instructed me to climb over.

Valerie gave me a boost up and I climbed up onto the top of the wall, it was no higher than 6 feet, and I dropped down the other side, endeavouring without much success to make as little sound as possible. Valerie joined me a moment later, landing with so little noise that she would have made the average cat feel that it was breaking noise abatement laws. We were in the middle of some low shrubs that screened the wall from what turned out to be a garden. A large house loomed up on our left. The front was in darkness, but a glow of light suggested that the back of the house might be a rewarding place to go and look at. Valerie read my thoughts. Taking my hand she led me around the edge of the garden towards the rear of the house, carefully staying in the shadows offered by the wall and the shrubbery. James Bond couldn't have done it better. I wondered where she had learned such skills in covert behaviour.

We moved down the side of the house to a point where we were able to look at the whole building from sideways on. A large conservatory like structure extended backwards from the brick built main building. This was the source of the light, as the structure's light pollution blotted out the stars. As we watched a man walked along the inside length of it. He wore only a pair of shorts. Even from this distance I could recognise Otto Langsdorf. He had put on a lot of weight since the photo that I had seen had been taken. He gave a whole new meaning to the term *bloated capitalist*. Turning, he called something along the length of the conservatory, then threw himself forward. I expected to see him cause himself serious injury when he landed, but instead he disappeared from view to be replaced by a giant splash of water. "Swimming Pool" the realisation hit me.

Valerie tugged at my arm. I turned and saw she was pointing towards the end of the garden, directly behind the house. I followed the line of her outstretched arm and saw what she was indicating. In the backwash of the light from the pool area I could see a tree house. Not one of those "Swallows and Amazons" types of tree house, made of salvaged planks and tattered canvas, perched high in the branches of a tree and reachable only by a frayed rope ladder and at great personal risk. This was one of those pre-built tree houses that are sold in garden centres, and which stand about 4 feet off the ground. We made our way towards it. It seemed to take ages, but at last we were able to climb the short wooden ladder and take refuge in the deep darkness inside.

Valerie dipped into her rucksack and took a couple of objects out. She handed the first to me. It turned out to be a pair of binoculars. I turned to the window space of the tree house, which gave a view to the front, over the lawns. Raising the binoculars to my eyes I focused them on the back of the house. The level of lighting in the pool area made everything inside stand out as clear as if it were a bright Summer's day.

Langsdorf had climbed out of the pool and was now being towelled dry by a pair of very obliging young ladies. They were dressed, if that's the right word, in bikini bottoms and nothing else. Another male figure was seated on a poolside lounger with another, similarly unclad woman draped across his lap. A third man sat at a barstool alongside a cocktail bar, with a girl on either side. I recognised him as David Trace. It didn't take a genius to work out who the man on the lounger was, even though his companion screened him from full view. It had to be Elgin, otherwise there was no reason for us to be here.

I felt movement as Valerie joined me at the window. I turned towards her and saw her lift some sort of camera to her eye. "Latest from Metro TV." She whispered. "Takes high quality video in almost any sort of light."

I returned my attention to the house. There was movement to the rear of the cocktail bar and three more people entered the pool area. A woman walked between two men. The woman was older than the other women present, by several years. I placed her around her late thirties. She was attractive in her way, and had a full, generous figure. It wasn't difficult to make this out, as she was dressed like the other women, naked except for bikini pants. Her swimming trunks clad male companions were somewhat different to the other men present, though. For a start they were young. The one on her right was black, the other was either Mediterranean by ancestry, or he spent a lot of time on sun beds. Both had physiques that told of many hours a day spent in gymnasiums. The woman had her arms draped round the wastes of both of them. At a word from her they broke free and dived into the water to swim a few energetic lengths.

"Elsa Peters." Valerie breathed. I had almost guessed as much. Elsa went behind the cocktail bar and rummaged around for a moment. She found what she was looking for and lifted it out. A plastic bag containing something white. I didn't need a second guess as to what it might be. She emptied the contents onto the bar and produced what appeared to be a credit card and started chopping at the powder. The other people gathered around her to watch what she was doing. I realised that apart from Elsa, none of the women was over twenty years of age, and a couple looked considerably younger than that. The two young studs climbed out of the pool and wandered over to join them all. They had shed their trunks while they were in the pool.

Nearly everyone took turns at snorting the cocaine, though I noticed that the two young men refrained. Valerie whispered her frustration as Elgin refused to turn around and give her a clear look at his face. When the last of the drug had been shared there seemed to be some discussion. 'Oh for a concealed microphone.' I thought. At last some decision was reached and there was a general movement out of the pool area. Lights came on upstairs to reveal a french window behind a wrought iron balcony.

Behind the glass of the window I could just make out figures moving as the room filled up. Two of the girls rose head and shoulders above the crowd and started bouncing up and down, probably on a bed. Pillows appeared in their hands and a pillow fight ensued. Someone must have sensed something, or at least decided there was a chance of being seen, as curtains were finally pulled across the window, concealing the rest of the evening's activities. We watched patiently for long time, long enough to witness two of the girls return to the pool area, naked now, and take a swim. Valerie said she didn't think we would see any one of direct interest to us anymore that night, and so we left as soon as we were sure we wouldn't be seen from inside the house.

We retraced our steps through the shrubbery and back over the wall, before assuming our disguise of late night (very late night) joggers.

As Valerie drove off I challenged her on what we had just seen.

"You knew that was going to happen, didn't you? That's why we came up this evening, and not in the morning."

"Not *knew*. Suspected more like. We picked up rumours of parties, but could never get any more than that. Swingers are a pretty secretive lot; all pseudonyms and friends of friends and friends of friends introductions. But we've got someone close to the local party organisation now. When I went back to my room I was waiting for a 'phone call. It came, and told me where to go. That's when I called you."

"Whose house is it? Langsdorf's?"

"No, Trace's. I told you he was living beyond his means. Its rented, but the rent is phenomenal, well beyond the capabilities of a retired tool fitter, even one who saved all his money and has a good pension. He claims to have made some good stock market investments,"

"Who have you got inside?" I remembered the third set of handwriting on the notes in the file.

"Sorry, need-to-know. Lets just say he's in a position to keep an eye on what goes on in Wroxborough." She paused as she negotiated the car through a bend in the road.

"I'm not sure I got a clean shot of Elgin's face. I'm afraid the night's been a bit of a wash-out, after all."

"Not at all," I contradicted her. "You must have got good clear footage of Elsa Peters. That must be worth something. She was naked, well virtually, with a couple of studs on her arm, and clearly involved in drug taking. If we can't use that then we don't deserve to get our story."

Valerie pondered this for a moment. "OK, but we mustn't squander this. It doesn't link Elgin to Trace, or the drugs, or the girls. Elsa Peters could just resign and leave Elgin virtually unharmed."

"OK, we won't do anything with the video until Steven's seen it." I agreed. "Then we can plan how best to use it."

We arrived back at the hotel and went our separate ways. I considered the night's events, not least the revelation that Steven, or was it Steven and Valerie? had someone on the inside of the local party, close enough to know where Elgin was going to be that evening.

*   *   *

Morning saw us arrive at the constituency party offices, which were located above the party member's social club. Elsa Peters, fully clothed and looking like a pillar of the establishment, greeted us and asked us to take seats in the small reception area.

Expensive make up almost totally disguised the ravages of the previous evening – almost. She herself sat behind a desk and proceeded to work her way through the morning post. She explained that Timothy, as she referred to him, had been delayed and would arrive shortly.

There must have been another entrance to the building, because it wasn't long before a young man came through the door from what must have been another office, to say that Timothy had arrived, and would see us in a moment. He carried a chauffeur's cap, which he hung on the coat rack. Sitting himself on a seat in the corner he pulled a paperback novel from his pocket. Immersing himself in his book he ignored us. He and my cat could have been soul mates.

The intercom buzzed, and Elsa Peters went through into the office. She returned a moment later, holding the door open as she asked us to go through. She closed the door behind us, and we were at last in The Presence. Timothy Elgin walked forward to greet us, smiling and offering his hand. It was the professional smile of someone who does a lot of meeting and greeting. It didn't touch his eyes. Elgin invited us over to a semi-circle of comfortable chairs, where a coffee pot and cups waited for us on a low table. He made small talk while he busied himself with pouring the coffee and offering biscuits.

At last he considered that there had been enough pleasantries, and turned our attention to business. I gave him a brief outline of the sort of programme that I was supposed to be producing; a weekly profile of major political figures, and we would be so pleased if he would be the first one we covered. He smiled as I massaged his ego a little. He had already agreed, of course, when Valerie had spoken to him on the telephone, but these niceties helped to oil the wheels. He gave his consent and asked what we wanted to know.

"Can we start" I opened, "with your early life, your family and influences?"

"Well, it was a fairly normal upbringing, I suppose. Depending how you define normal, of course." His smile twinkled, but still didn't reach his eyes. "My father was a solicitor here in Wroxborough, and my mother was an usher at the Magistrate's Court. They met, of course, when my father attended the court on business. They started seeing each other, and married about a year later. I came along about 18 months after the wedding. I'm an only child, but my parents never seemed to want more children. Of course in those days women didn't pursue *careers*, as such, and so my mother stayed at home to look after me. Dad became a partner in one of the leading solicitor's firms in the town, so they were invited to all the major events, which is how I got to know so many of the influential people in local politics. Dad had no interest in politics himself though."

He paused and took a sip of his coffee. "I went to the local primary school, and was fortunate enough to go on to the St Edward's, the local Grammar School. Competition was stiff, as you can imagine in a town this size, with only one Grammar. I got 10 GCSE's, all at grade A and B, and then 5 A levels, that was 4 A's and one B. Oxford took me no problem at all." I had most of this from the research I had done, as his exam successes had been thought worthy of reporting in the local papers. It was interesting to hear him talk about it though. He told us of his results as though they were the not only expected, but had been taken for granted. "At Oxford I read Politics and Economics, and came away with a double First."

"What was it that first interested you in politics?" I asked as he drew breath.

"That started at St Edwards. In the third year there was a General Election. Maggie Thatcher versus Neil Kinnock, round two. Our English teacher thought it would be a good idea to hold a mock election. I was chosen as one candidate, and one of the girls was chosen as the other. I'm sorry to say I lost. One of my policies was that children should do chores around the house to earn their pocket money, and that didn't go down too well with my classmates. Besides which Karen, the other candidate, was snogging half the boys in the class, and I couldn't compete with that."

He smiled, but it was obvious that this seemingly unimportant event had touched him in some way. I could also see how such a lesson was learnt and used in later life. "However, I was bitten by the campaigning bug, and that stimulated my interest in politics as a generic subject. From there I got involved in various school activities, such as the Debating Society, and continued that when I went to University. I was a leading light in the *Union*, both as an events organiser and as a debater. I invited our local MP to join us one evening. Ultimately that led to me being offered a job as his researcher, though that was a couple of years later. He had just been appointed as a junior Foreign Office Minister, and needed more resource, which was fortunate for me."

The interview continued in this vein for some time, with me asking fairly simple questions and Elgin blowing his own trumpet a lot. No one would ever accuse him of being too modest. While Valerie scribbled her notes I watched Elgin carefully. He was at ease with us, entirely in his comfort zone and in control, but I could tell that he was never totally open. He wasn't sufficiently relaxed, as though a part of his mind was on guard duty, making sure that nothing slipped out unnoticed. At last I thanked him for his time and we left the office. We stopped by Elsa Peter's desk and thanked her for her time. She looked tired, which was unsurprising. Nodding to the chauffeur, who continued to ignore us, we made our way down the narrow stairs.

"Look, I've got a few things I want to look into, while we're up here." I said to Valerie. "Why don't you head off back to London, and I'll catch a later train."

"Anything I should know about?" she asked.

"No, nothing major." Why did that question make me feel that she was the boss, and I the underling? "Just a few things that Timothy said that I want to follow up on, check out the local papers, again, that sort of thing."

We agreed to meet the following day, and then said our goodbyes. Valerie headed off to the taxi office on the first leg of her homeward journey. I waited until she was out of sight, then turned back towards the constituency offices. I didn't go up the stairs, I went instead into the social club, the fund raising arm of the local party.

Four elderly men sat at a table on the far side of the room, playing a game of dominoes and sipping at halves of bitter. The only other person present was the barman, who was making a career out of polishing a pint glass.

"Elsa said it would be OK if I popped in for a drink, even though I'm not a member." I lied to the barman. He stopped polishing the glass and reached for another from behind the bar. "I'll have a pint of lager, if I may." I continued. "Tell you what, why not have one yourself?"

Four hours and several pints later I caught the train back to London, satisfied that I had achieved more than I had expected to when I left Timothy Elgin's office. I wondered why I felt this way. True, I had found out that a member of the British Government had been a participant in a sex and drugs orgy, but that wasn't what had led to my involvement in the first place.

Why had I been so ready to believe that an elected public servant, whose image was snowy white, could be involved in the sort of corruption that was the hallmark of some third world banana republic? After all, it isn't as if we were confronted with such goings on every day of our lives. As I gazed through the window of the train it hit me between the eyes.

The train was trundling through the outskirts of Wroxborough at about 30 mph. Through the window I could see a scene that was typical of most large towns and cities. It was a cluster of three tower blocks, surrounded by some lower level blocks of flats, like chicks around mother hens, only far less wholesome. Many windows were covered up with graffiti daubed chip board. Elsewhere broken glass sparkled in the weak sunlight. A burnt out car stood on its axles on a weed grown patch of grass and mud. School age children hung around on the corner of a street, instead of being sat in classrooms as they should have been. Someone had made a conscious decision to build this monstrosity, I realised. Someone had decided to knock down the horizontal slums that had skirted the city, and replaced them, not with pleasant streets and houses, but with vertical chicken coops into which families could be shoe horned; out of sight and out of mind. It is said that if you confine too many rats in too small a space they will start to fight and kill each other. The evidence before my eyes suggested that humans might have a similar tendency.

The train slowed to a standstill, the third unscheduled stop since we had left the station. The privatised rail service that had replaced British Rail had failed to do what the government had said it would do. The government unable, or unwilling, to make Britain's trains run on time had handed the problem to private industry. That private industry could do no better came as no surprise. The train I sat in was cleaner and more modern than its BR predecessor, but the infrastructure that supported it was still so poor that it meant it still ran late, or sometimes didn't run at all.

The incompetence of elected officials was everywhere to be seen. In the hospitals, in the schools, in the housing, in the transport. So, if these people weren't able to fix what was so obviously broken there had to be another reason for them seeking election, didn't there? Politics, I concluded, was self interest raised to an art form. And where there's self interest it is only to be expected that there would, under the surface, be corruption. Had I always known this? Perhaps. I reeled off the names: Profumo, Stonehouse, Lambton, Hamilton, Aitken, Archer. And they were just the ones who had resigned or gone to prison. What of all those who had brazened it out? What of the ones who had resigned, spent a short period in the wilderness and then returned to office all the stronger now they were seen to be indispensable? The ones who hid behind House of Commons privilege, or who had persuaded others to lie on their behalf in order to effect a cover up. Of course, that couldn't be proven, could it? To make allegations against a named person would attract a libel suit quicker than a politician's denial. And that, of course, was what Timothy Elgin was relying on. If you can't afford to lose a court case, you won't risk saying anything in public. QED.

It might be assumed from this conclusion that I am some sort of anarchist, but this couldn't be further from the truth. Any group of people, call it a society, needs some sort of governing body to make sure that the rights and privileges of the many aren't subverted by the few for their own ends. When, however, it is the guardians of those rights that are doing the subverting, then it becomes the responsibility of the many to bring them back to heel. It is, after all, us that pay their wages. Who pays the piper calls the tune. But who guards the guardians?

I started to feel that glow of moral indignation which we lesser mortals always feel when we believe we have right on our side. If I had known what the cost would be I would have thrown myself out of the train there and then. At least I would have if it had managed to get to a speed that would cause some sort of injury when I landed.

I returned my attention to the evening newspaper. The lead story was of a politician who denied using his influence to smooth the path to British citizenship for a wealthy foreign businessman. He had the full backing of the Prime Minister. Well, there's a surprise.

CHAPTER SIX

We sat in Steven's lounge viewing the video footage that Valerie had taken two nights earlier. Just as Valerie had suspected, she hadn't caught a clear and identifiable view of Timothy Elgin.

"I like the idea of using the video against Peters, though." Said Steven.

"Won't work, I'm afraid." I offered my opinion. "You'll get nothing out of Peters."

"How can you be so sure? You were all for it the other night?" Valerie was puzzled.

"New information. As Valerie knows, I spent some time in Wroxborough yesterday afternoon, but the subject of my research wasn't Elgin, as I led you to believe, but Peters." I paused, building up my moment of glory.

"Well?" they both exclaimed.

"Elsa Peters married someone called Gary Peters about 20 years ago. The marriage was short lived. He went off with another woman, leaving Elsa with a baby, to fend for herself. She didn't suffer though, because she had wealthy relatives. At least they were to become wealthy. Elsa's maiden name was Langsdorf." I revealed, like a conjurer pulling rabbit from a hat. "She's Otto's sister."

The two of them pondered on this information. "You don't think she would betray Elgin because she's Otto's sister." concluded Steven.

"If Elgin goes down Otto is almost certain to go down with him. Seeing them all together the other night suggests they're a close knit group. I doubt she would willingly sell her brother out." Its a pity I'm not a better judge of character. "If we confront her she can resign leaving Elgin in the clear – and very angry."

"There's still Trace." Interjected Valerie. "We've got him on video too."

"Small fry." I suggested. "What have we got? Having semi-clad people round for a party isn't a crime, and we can't prove he provided the drugs, as Elsa is the one seen opening the packet. The best we've got is him allowing his house to be used for the taking of drugs, for which the maximum he's likely to get is a caution. If we went to him with that he'd laugh at us. He's retired now, so doesn't have a reputation to worry about." I let this sink in. "The fourth person there, Otto, we have nothing against at all. He isn't even married, so we couldn't even threaten to show his wife the video. We can try to kick up a bit of a stink, but these people aren't household names. There's too little to be gained"

"What about Elgin's wife, we could threaten to show her the video, and suggest that the fourth person is her husband. That might persuade Elgin to co-operate." Valerie was desperate to salvage something from our nocturnal adventure.

"Won't work." Steven seemed certain. "The black guy. We've seen him before, in one of our photographs. He's a bouncer at a night club, but he makes extra money as a male escort. He's been seen at Elgin's house in Wroxborough. The suggestion is that

Camilla Elgin hires him for sex, and further, that Elgin himself has joined in the fun. I think we can conclude that their marriage is fairly open in those terms, so there's no pressure we can apply from that direction. There is one thing we can do, and that is to reveal that we know about the party, and hope that it gets Elgin running scared. Clarke, what plans have you for the book?"

"I've decided on a format, but haven't actually started work on any of the content yet. I've decided to do it in the form of flash backs. Each chapter will open with the principle character, I'm calling him Gerald Dempsey, talking to someone about his life, which then cuts to a flash back of the actual events. Obviously the dialogue will be imaginary, but everything will be based on things which we know took place. At the end the reader will find out that Dempsey is talking to his barrister, who is preparing a plea of mitigation for Dempsey, following guilty verdicts on a whole raft of charges. Its not highly original, but it works."

"That sounds good. I like the idea of Dempsey telling the story himself. It will add that extra grain of veritas. Can you work up a first draft on what you saw at Trace's house?"

"That should be quite easy, as I witnessed the whole thing. It will take a me a week or so, I should think. Why, what are you planning?"

"Well, while you and Valerie were in the Midlands I went to see an old college friend of mine. She has always had a yen for me, poor deluded girl, but we've always stayed friends. Anyway, she works for one of the Daily's now, and she's agreed to act as the channel for us to leak news of the book. She will plant the bait, and then presumably she will be approached in order to try to identify us. Then we'll use her to feed the story to Elgin, and others, and hopefully the hares will start running. I've already set things in motion, and she will be planting a little item in one of the political diaries which should catch Elgin's eye. We'll see where we go from there when we see what sort of reaction we get."

I agreed to provide a rough draft that covered the pool party, for the following week, and the meeting broke up. I noticed that Valerie was quite cool towards me, as though I had upset her in some way. I concluded that she hadn't taken kindly to me not involving her in my *research* in Wroxborough, but I couldn't quite understand why she should be so upset. I put it out of my mind as I went home in the taxi. I had decided to get my own back on my cat by ignoring it. It didn't seem to notice it was being ignored.

*   *   *

Timothy Elgin sat in his office in the Palace of Westminster. It was a large office, as befitted his status as Deputy Prime Minister. His feet were propped up on the corner of an antique oak desk, as he read his way through the daily papers. Each morning he had a press briefing from his advisors, prioritised by stories about him, stories about the party and stories about the government, in that order. However, he did enjoy reading the news first hand as well, so that he could get the full flavour of what was being said. His eyes lit on a small item at the bottom of one of the diary columns. It hadn't been mentioned in his press briefing.

Rumours are rife about a new book which threatens to blow the whistle on a major political career. The book is said to contain revelations about major wrong doing by a senior politician, thinly disguised as fiction. Having seen just about every sort of scandal that politics throws up, this columnist can't wait to read what new revelations there might be.

Elgin reached towards his office 'phone to summon his Press Advisor, but stopped short. Perhaps this was the time for discretion. Instead he fished his mobile 'phone out of his pocket and keyed through the 'phone book until he found the number he was looking for. He didn't waste any time on preamble.

"Usual place. 2.00 pm" he commanded, and broke the connection.

Later that day he called for his car. The title of Deputy Prime Minister isn't an official one, so Elgin wasn't entitled to an official car, but a grateful party was pleased to pay for one for him. He instructed the driver to take him to the Burlington Arcade, where he got out at the Piccadilly entrance and dismissed the car. He walked slowly through the arcade, taking time to stop and look in the windows of the shops, before emerging into Burlington Gardens at the other end. Satisfied that he wasn't being watched Elgin hailed a cab and directed it to a pub in Shepherds Market. The man he was due to meet was already sat in a corner booth.

Elgin wasted no time with greetings. He took out his wallet and produced the cutting of the press article that he was concerned about. He gave the man the cutting and waited while he read through it, sipping at the scotch and soda that the man had bought for him prior to his arrival.

"What do you want me to do?" asked the man, when he had finished reading.

"I want to know who's writing the book, and who the subject of the book is. And I want to know quickly."

"Shouldn't be a problem." Replied the man. "I'll get back to you in a couple of days."

"Two days." Instructed Elgin, "no more."

Elgin left, and used his mobile to tell his chauffeur to meet him back at the Burlington Arcade.

Two days later the two men met again, in the same pub.

"I spoke to a journo who works on the column this appeared in." the man explained. "She said she had got the story from a man at a party. She said he wouldn't go into detail, but promised she would get the exclusive when the book was about to come out. She thought at first he was just trying to chat her up, but he seemed so earnest that she started to believe him. Kept on saying that the book would rip Westminster wide open. He wouldn't say who the book was about though."

"No clue at all as to who the subject of the book was?" Elgin asked.

"None at all. But I've got her to promise to pass on anything else she gets. I've promised her an exclusive of my own if she cooperates." He grinned. "That and the couple of hundred I bunged her should keep her sweet."

"OK, keep in touch with her. I want to know as soon as she gets anything else."

"Worried, are you, Mr Elgin?"

"Keep your voice down." Hissed Elgin. "I don't want the whole pub knowing who I am. And yes, I am worried, and so should you be. Remember who pays your wages."

With that Elgin threw back the remains of his whisky and left the pub.

*   *   *

"We've had a nibble." Valerie reported over the 'phone. "Sam Walker, that's Steven's love struck journo friend. She was in the pub the journo's use after work when a guy turned up, asking questions about the diary column item. Eventually someone pointed her out. He told her that he might have some information that would be of use in the book, but obviously needed to know who the author was. Sam played it dumb, said she wasn't sure of the name of the author. Our cover story is that a bloke started blabbing to her at a party. The only reason she believed him at all was that he sounded so sincere. Anyway, she agreed that if the bloke, the author, got in touch again she would contact this guy. She was given a couple of hundred for her trouble, which she's going to donate to a children's charity. I think our fox is sniffing the air"

I agreed with Valerie. £200 isn't idle curiosity. "The draft chapter's ready." I reported. What shall I do with it?"

"E-mail it to Steven. I'll set up a meeting between him and Sam and he'll pass it on."

*   *   *

It was a few days later that Elgin sat at the breakfast table in the London flat that he shared with his wife. The flat was too small for a family, so Elgin's daughters were sent off to boarding school. Camilla came in with the morning post and laid it on the breakfast table at Elgin's elbow. She took a seat and poured herself tea from the pot on the table.

Elgin laid aside the Cabinet Briefing Paper he had been reading and picked up the mail. He leafed through it until he reached the large packet that was on the bottom of the pile. He examined the handwriting on the address and decided that the packet was important enough for him to open immediately.

Elgin slit the envelope with his butter knife and pulled out the wad of A4 paper that was enclosed. A hand written Post-it note was stuck to the top sheet, to inform him that the letter was from Scott Davis, the man that Elgin had met in the pub.

Elgin read through the sheets of paper, his eyes starting to bulge and his jaw drop as he turned from page to page. His tea went cold in the cup in front of him, his toast lay untouched.

"Shouldn't you be leaving for Number 10, dear?" asked Camilla, without looking up from the morning paper. Surprised by the lack of response, she glanced up to see the expression on Elgin's face. "My God, you look like you've seen a ghost."

Elgin tore his eyes from the page he had been reading. "I wish it was a ghost." Whispered Elgin, his throat was dry with panic. "This could ruin us."

"What do you mean?" realisation dawned. "I thought you said you were untouchable."

"It seems that I might not be. Remember the last time I went up to Wroxborough, I said I'd been to a party at that dick-head Trace's?"

"Yes, you told me about it. Quite a night you said it had been. That reminds me…."

"That's what this is about." Interrupted Elgin. "It looks like its going to be written up as part of a book of some sort." Elgin handed the papers over to his wife. "Read it for yourself."

Camilla Elgin read through the thin sheaf of papers. She had been to Trace's house and recognised the description of it. She also recognised the descriptions of the other people there, even though the names that were given to them meant nothing to her. When she finished she handed the papers back. Elgin told her about the newspaper item that had attracted his attention. "Its me the book is about." He confessed. "And if they can get it published it will open up a whole can of worms."

"But its fiction. It can't be linked to you."

"Don't be so sure. It only needs one person to come forward and say that they are Fred so-and-so or Mary this-and-that, a name used in the book, and the whole thing will go public. They start to tell what they know, and the reptiles do the rest. The police could even get involved, and if they start digging it won't be long before people start making deals in order to save their own skins." He banged his fist on the table, causing the crockery to jump and rattle.

"It doesn't mean it will implicate you. They've called the politician Gerald Dempsey. OK, so the description makes him sound a bit like you, but then it could sound like just about anyone, including the Prime Minister." She giggled. "Its a good thing they didn't get a look at your birth mark."

"This is no laughing matter." Snapped Elgin, but he too had thought the same. His birth mark was very small but very distinctive, shaped very like a lion, and it would have identified him as surely as a fingerprint to anyone that had ever seen him naked. That was quite a few people, one way or another.

"You didn't tell me Elsa Peters was there." Accused Camilla. Unlike the prostitutes that were hired in for the parties, Camilla considered Elsa Peters something of a threat to her marriage.

"Don't worry about Elsa, she's a friend. And she invited herself. Besides, Elsa's been good to us. Without her we wouldn't have got nearly as far with this as we have. She's the lynch pin in just about every deal, and she's the one that makes sure my fingerprints aren't on things. She also knows where the bodies are buried, so we have to keep her sweet." Elgin saw the angry look on his wife's face. "Don't worry. Elsa doesn't mean anything to me, not in that way, and I'd never let her come between us." He paused, building up to a more robust argument. "You didn't seem to mind Elsa when you were having sex with her."

"That was different." Slightly mollified, Camilla turned to more practical matters. "What are you going to do about it?" asked Camilla, concerned for the future of herself and her family.

"The only thing I can do." replied Elgin. "Make sure that the book is never published."

CHAPTER SEVEN

I was talking to Steven on the 'phone. "We have to get more on the corruption side of things, especially the local Government stuff. I want to speak to Daphne Gibson."

"Do you think she'll talk? asked Steven.

"I have no idea, but if we don't get something a bit more solid than we've got, I won't be able to produce a credible book. I need to crack an eye witness, and Daphne seems the most likely candidate. She and her husband are living well beyond their means out in Portugal, so I might be able to open a crack by attacking their lifestyle."

"OK," Agreed Steven, "but you're paying for your own air fares."

I already had. I switched off my mobile and headed for the British Airways check-in desk.

*   *   *

I drove the hire car up the hill towards the villa, the only building along this cart track that passed itself off as a road. Away to one side the view spread out across the coastal resorts to the Atlantic Ocean, glittering in the sunlight. With a view like that I wasn't surprised that property prices around these parts were so high.

I returned my eyes to the road just in time to avoid the gate post that marked the boundary between the public *highway* and the private property of the villa. A sign announced that this was Wroxborough Lodge.

Daphne Gibson herself answered the solid, if rather ornate wooden door. She greeted me with a smile, but it soon dissolved into a frown as she read the business card (fake) that announced me as a Peter Wesley, journalist for a particularly down market British tabloid newspaper. However, British working class manners overcame her distaste and she invited me in and offered me tea. While she bustled off to sort this out I was able to take in my surroundings.

The villa was very much an English person's idea of a Spanish hacienda and totally ignored the Moorish influences that dominate the architecture of this part of Southern Portugal. Earthenware jugs and ethnic rugs dominated the decor, along with very English touches of rose print cushion covers and antique silver picture frames. Daphne returned with the tea things.

Life hadn't been kind to Daphne, I could see. She looked older than her 62 years, and each line on her face told the story of a battle fought or a disappointment endured. I was expecting someone who was overweight, which the last 'photo I had seen strongly suggested, but instead I found a woman that was frail to the point that she looked ill. I almost regretted what I had come to do, but I reminded myself that this sad middle aged woman had taken bribes, and perhaps worse, which made her a criminal. I steeled myself and launched into my first question.

"What can you tell me about the Long Bottom Farm planning application?"

"I don't know what you mean." Daphne immediately went onto the defensive. "That was a perfectly normal planning application, which was handled in the normal manner."

"Hardly normal, Mrs Gibson." I persisted. "The land was zoned for agriculture, yet ended up as an industrial estate as a result of your committee giving its approval."

"The zoning change went before the full Council, in the normal manner, and they agreed to change its use from agricultural to industrial. I was only one councillor, you know, I couldn't change zoning rules on my own."

"The Council minutes show you proposing the change Mrs Gibson."

"But the full council still had to vote, so the change wasn't down to me."

"OK, Mrs Gibson. Lets forget Long Bottom Farm for a moment. What about the High Cliff Retirement Home?" She flinched visibly as I said the name.

"Again, a routine application for the demolition of the building and the building of some apartments."

"Not just apartments, Mrs Gibson, top of the range luxury apartments. And all those old people made homeless, who had to go into Council care instead."

"All routine and above board, all the same."

I decided that a change of tack might be in order. I made a show of admiring the room we were sitting in.

"A lovely place you have here, Mrs Gibson. If you'll forgive me saying so, it seems a bit beyond the means of a retired milkman."

"How dare you. My Will was a good provider. We never went hungry." She stood and left the room, returning a moment later. Angrily she thrust several sheets of paper at me. "My Will was really good at picking the horses. There you are, every bet he ever placed, the dates, the racecourse, the odds, everything."

I looked down at the closely typed pages, which showed, supposedly, racing bets going back nearly 30 years. It provided a neat explanation. Too neat. A professional gambler might keep records like that, but not an amateur.

"These can be traced back through the bookmakers, you know." I persisted.

"On track betting, Mr Wesley. It can't be traced."

"Very convenient, Mrs Gibson." I tried my final throw of the dice. "Have you a DVD player?" She said she had, so I handed her the pool party DVD and asked her to play it. She went into another room. I opted to stay where I was. She was back a few minutes later, clearly distressed.

"Get this filth out of my house." She spat. "I'll thank you to leave now." To emphasise the point she walked to the big front door and threw it open. "If you come back here again I'll 'phone the police." She shouted, as she slammed the door behind me.

I don't know how I had expected the meeting to turn out, but I felt deflated. I had several hours before my return flight was due to leave, so to cheer myself up I decided to do a little sight seeing. I drove down to Villamourra and parked by the marina. Villamourra is a modern town built specifically for the tourist industry, and the marina is surrounded on three sides by expensive shops, café's and bars. I indulged myself with the sort of ice cream that one only eats on holiday.

I was just tucking into my sticky feast when my mobile 'phone chirped into life.

"This is Daphne Gibson." Said the voice on the other end. "Are you still in Portugal?"

I said that I was. "Good. Look, I've changed my mind. I will talk to you. Come back up to the villa." I told her I would be no more than half an hour. Abandoning my ice cream I almost ran to my car. 40 minutes later I was once again avoiding the gate posts of Wroxborough Lodge.

Daphne Gibson must have heard the approach of my car, as she was stood at the door. We went inside and she enacted the tea ceremony once again. I could see that she was distressed; going through some inner torment. Red around her eyes suggested she had been crying.

I let her take her time. If she had decided to talk then she would get to the point if left her to herself. At last she spoke.

"Will was a milkman, Summer and Winter, rain or shine, for 40 years. It was the rain that got him, of course. Chronic bronchitis. He was in and out of hospital all the time. A week here, a fortnight there. And if he didn't work he didn't get paid. We were as poor as church mice, even after the kids left home. It was a good hospital in those days, nice nurses and doctors, but always short of cash, as they are. I got involved in charity work, raising money for hospital funds. That was when I met him first, Timothy Elgin." She spoke his name with sadness, as though she had put faith in him and he had let her down.

"It was at some charity do. I wasn't used to those sort of things: a bit of a fish out of water. He talked to me for a while and he seemed so nice. Anyway, I was just leaving when that woman, Elsa Peters" she almost spat after she said the name, "She came up to me. She seemed so nice then as well. Anyway, she suggested I might stand for the Council. Said I was obviously a good organiser and my heart was in the right place. She said I could do a lot of good for the hospital if I was on the council. She really laid it on thick. I was flattered I suppose, so I talked to Will about it. He was off work again, so we had lots of time to chat. He said I should go for it, and that was the decision made.

Anyway, it had been 50 years since my ward had returned one of the other lot, so I walked in at the election. I was hardly through the door of the Council Offices before the Leader was asking me to Chair the planning committee. I protested, of course, said I wouldn't know what to do, but he wouldn't have it. Said the Head of Planning would look after me and tell me all I needed to know. Anyway, that was that, and a week later I was at my first Planning Committee meeting. And the Leader was off on a fortnight's holiday that I found out later someone else had paid for." Daphne sipped at her tea, her eyes downcast to the saucer resting on her lap. She composed herself to continue. I stayed silent. She seemed almost to be in a trance.

"Anyway, not much happened for a while, then Elsa Peters came to me and said she needed my help. A local party big-wig was having trouble with a neighbour. Wanted to build an extension to his house, and the neighbours were objecting because it would cast a shadow on their garden. Could I make sure the planning application went through all right, because the party owed this person a few favours? I wasn't happy, but I could hardly say no, I didn't know how to. Anyway, I persuaded the other committee members that no one had the right to dictate to their neighbours, and made sure it went through, and then a few days later I got a telephone call telling me to meet a man in a pub. His name is Scott Davis, by the way." She said, acknowledging my presence for the first time since she had started talking.

"I met him, and he handed me an envelope. When I opened it I found £200 inside. 'A little thank you from someone,' he said it was. I tried to give it back, but he wouldn't take it. Said it was mine by rights, and that if I didn't take it the man would be insulted and that would be bad for the party. So I took it. Anyway, that was the start of it. Funny thing was, the application was all legal and above board. Casting a shadow on your neighbour's property isn't grounds for refusal. I didn't have to do anything at all really."

"After that was the Long Bottom Farm business. I was given some money which I had to spread around a few people, Council officials, Councillors, you know. They all took it without a murmur.

The re-zoning went through, I got the planning application passed, and that was that. A week later I was back in the pub with another envelope in my hand with two grand in it. I'd never seen so much money." She started to weep a little, but managed to get herself under control once again.

"There were others, a grand here and two grand there. In fact we never got more than about 20 thousand all told. My Will was good with money though. All that time in hospital he'd started reading the financial pages of the newspapers, with so much time on his hands. Then the investment journals, so he really did know what he was talking about. We still couldn't explain the initial stake money though, so that's when Elsa Peters came up with the horse racing story as a cover. She got me all the names and dates and everything, for past races, then all I had to do was go through the papers each day and get the results from the previous day, and pick out a few high paying winners. The investments she did for us, through *off shore nominees*." She said the phrase like someone who had learnt it by heart. "whatever they are. Of course we never paid tax on any of it, only commission to the nominees. It soon mounted up. My Will really was good." She said it proudly.

"He got into Dot Coms when they were just starting out, and got out before they crashed. He got out of Railtrack, though we got a tip off about that one. He got out of Enron. He seemed to be able to read the future when it came to the stock markets. Anyway, we bought this bit of land and had the villa built, as somewhere to retire to, so that Will wouldn't have to suffer the damp ever again. It was good for his bronchitis, you know, this place." She paused as tears returned to her eyes again. "He died just a couple of weeks ago, though, and he's left me on my own out here. And those bastards, sorry, I shouldn't swear. Those people didn't even come to the funeral. Not even a wreath." She sobbed for a moment, then pushed herself into continuing.

"Then there was High Cliff. I really didn't want to do that one. I said no. But that Scott Davis came round to the house. He showed me pictures, taken in the pub. Me taking the envelopes, me counting the money. Me putting the envelopes in my hand bag. Told me he'd send them to the police if I didn't play ball, as he put it. I had no choice. Anyway, that was the last one I did. I resigned from the Council after that and we moved out here." She wiped her nose with a tissue.

"If you'd started looking into those horse races you'd have soon tumbled things weren't right. It seemed like a good cover. Milkmen always have their afternoons free, so plenty of time to go racing. But for half those races Will was in hospital, and you can't bet *on track* from a hospital bed." She fell silent at last.

"What about the maintenance contracts?" I asked.

"Oh, you know about those as well do you. I was only ever a go-between for those. I got the tender information from the finance office and passed it to Elgin. He gave me a back hander, some of which I passed on to the clerk in the Finance Department as a little *present*. That Scott Davis was up to his neck in that business. He'd go round to the building companies and threaten them, tell them not bid, or to withdraw their bids. One of them wouldn't play ball, and he got beaten up with baseball bats. He never worked again. He died a year later." She wept at the memory.

"Why are you telling me all this now?" I asked. I kept my voice low, sympathetic.

"We're Catholics, Will and me. He knew he was dying and didn't want to go with all those sins on his conscience. We have an English speaking priest in Villamourra, so Will asked him to hear his confession. The priest gave him absolution, but told him that for the sin to be fully purged he had to own up, to confess his sins publicly. Well, they weren't his sins, really, they were mine. So now I'm owning up. I spoke to the priest, after you went earlier. He told me it was the right thing to do."

"Will you give evidence in court?" I asked hopefully.

Daphne smiled. "I suppose I'll have to, once you make this public."

I tied up a few loose ends. Daphne knew of other Councillors who had taken bribes, and I needed the names of them. She also knew of Councillors in other districts that Elgin and Peters had corrupted. I realised that in reality I hadn't established much of a case against Elgin. It was really against Peters and this Scott Davis character, but the rest would come, I was sure. At last I was certain the Daphne had told me everything that she could.

I said my farewells and assured her she was doing the right thing. I headed back to the airport. I wish I had taken Daphne with me.

On the flight back I started scribbling notes for my next chapter, and commenced work on it as soon as I got in the front door. I didn't even remember to collect my cat until Lilly brought it around. It growled at me and ran under the bed.

*   *   *

A week later Steven Rycroft left a rather smart restaurant in London's Soho. He had just lunched with Sam Walker, before handing over the latest draft chapter of the book for her to pass on. He hailed a taxi.

From further along the street a motor cycle pulled out and followed the taxi all the way to Fulham. It was the same motor cycle that had followed Sam Walker to the restaurant. As Rycroft shut his front door behind himself the motorcyclist pulled over to the curb and removed her crash helmet. She pulled a mobile 'phone from one of the many pockets of her leathers and speed dialled a number.

Scott Davis scribbled down the address that the girl gave him. "Good girl Tracy. You can go home and cook me up some dinner now." An hour later Davis had a name to go with the address.

CHAPTER EIGHT

"The shit's really hit the fan down at Metro." Steven told me, as I arrived for another of our meetings. "Elgin's been onto the Managing Editor, asking after a certain producer. Of course they denied having heard of you. Good job you used a fake name, by the way." He led me up to the office, where Valerie was busy at her computer.

"Anyway, there's a full scale inquiry going on to see if anyone at Metro was involved."

"Will they find that there was?" I asked.

"No, Valerie was far too clever for that. She only used a mobile 'phone, which everyone uses these days. Pay-as-you-go, which she threw away when we had finished with it. No, you're safe, Valerie's safe, and most importantly I'm safe." He settled himself into his swivel chair. "That new draft went off to Elgin today, according to Sam. He should have it in the morning, Royal Mail permitting."

"Have we got anywhere with Trace?" I asked.

"He's not playing at present. He's seen the video, of course, and so we must assume that Elgin has as well by now. But he's not biting yet. We enclosed a £20 note and told him if he wanted more then he was to place an ad in the personal column of the Wroxborough Chronicle. He hasn't done it this week, so we'll have to wait and see what happens next week."

With little more to go on for the moment I started to outline my ideas for some of the other chapters in the book.

"We've plenty of incriminating stuff from his time as a County Councillor, and that is good, but we really need something that's going grab national headlines. We need more on his connections to those Government contracts."

"Well, we know that he has links to business." Steven responded.

"Yes, but so has half the Cabinet. If that were a crime we could never elect a Government of any description." I hurried on. "We really need to find some fingerprints on a dodgy deal if we are going to make a plausible case."

"Perhaps we're tackling this from the wrong end." Valerie mused. "We'll have as much difficulty persuading a Civil Servant or a politician to spill the beans as we are having with local government people. No one wants to admit their guilt, in case they end up in court, or get the sack." She let us ponder on that for a moment, but she had clearly already thought this through. "What we really need is to turn this around. Instead of looking for a way in to expose Elgin's successful deals, we need to look for a failure."

"How do you mean?" I asked, very puzzled.

"I think I'm with you." Steven interjected. "Elgin may have tried to set up a deal that wasn't successful, where his business friends didn't get the contract. If so then someone in the Government, or the Civil Service, will know about it. However, because they didn't bite they don't have to fear prosecution. They may, therefore, be more willing to talk to us. That at least will tell us how they work, and we can look for the fingerprints on other deals."

"OK, I can see how that would work. How do we go about it?"

"You're the researcher. I suggest you go through all the material you have, check out his business contacts and eliminate them using the list of contracts we already have. That will leave us a short list of possibles. From that we work out which bit of Government they might have tried to deal with. Then its down to a little bribery of our own. We take a few Civil Service Press Officers to lunch, ply them with enough wine to get them talking, and see what they let slip."

"It sounds a bit hit and miss." I criticised.

Valerie broke in. "It is, but its all we've got. Are you willing to give it a go?"

"Looks like I don't have a lot of choice." I responded. "OK, I'll see what I can come up with.

*   *   *

Timothy and Camilla Elgin were sitting in their lounge watching the TV set, something they did infrequently. David Trace sat nervously on the edge of a hardback chair, waiting for some comment from them. He hadn't been made welcome, but they had listened to what he had to say.

The DVD ended and the picture reverted to its menu page, and showed a freeze frame of a girl walking down the side of the swimming pool.

"It didn't show a clear picture of you, Tim." Said Camilla. "Nothing that would stand up in court. Except perhaps Tyrone." She giggled.

Elgin shot his wife a venomous look. "No, but we know how they got the information now, don't we Trace? You had spies in your garden. Haven't you heard of security?"

David Trace mumbled his apologies, and tried to make excuses, but Elgin cut him off.

"Who was that other lovely boy, the Latin looking one?" inquired Camilla.

"Can't you keep your mind on the problem." Snapped Elgin. "We've more important things to think about than your next shag." Camilla pouted and lapsed into a sulky silence. Elgin stood up and went to a bureau and drew some papers out of a drawer. He handed them to Trace, who read them in silence.

"Bloody hell." He said at last. "That Daphne, I knew she wouldn't keep her mouth shut. I always said ……"

"You never said anything." Cut in Elgin. "You were just happy to take your cut and play Mr Big Time."

"What are we going to do about Daphne?" asked Trace.

"Leave Daphne to me." he replied. "I'll persuade her to be reasonable. I'm sure Otto would be prepared to part with a few thousand to keep her quiet." He stared Trace in the eye. "What about you?"

"Well, Mr Elgin, er Timothy." He wheedled. "You know you can rely on me to keep my mouth shut." He paused, summoning the courage to say what he wanted to say. "Of course money's getting tight. I could do with a bit more myself you know."

"You little shit." Spat Elgin. He leapt up and grabbed Trace by the lapels, half hauling him to his feet. "So that's why you've come, to try and put the bite on me."

"No, no Mr Elgin." Denied Trace. "I wouldn't do that to you. But people are going need paying off if I'm to keep this quiet. Word's bound to get out. We don't know if this is the only copy of the DVD. There's all those tarts to pay off, and the two boys. I haven't got that kind of money, not any more." Elgin saw the sense of his argument and released him.

"And if you can stuff a few notes in your back pocket, so much the better." Elgin sneered. But he saw the truth of what Trace was saying. "OK, I'll talk to Otto. But in the meantime I suggest you take a little holiday. Whoever sent you that recording expects you to get in contact with them, and when you don't they may arrive on your doorstep. After all," Elgin sneered, "they know where you live. Meet Davis at Heathrow tomorrow. He'll have tickets for you. A fortnight in Malaga better make you forgetful. Davis will contact you with the details."

"Can I take Lucy, you know the little redhead ….."

"Don't push your luck, Trace. Give Scott the names and addresses of the tarts. He'll spread the money around. He'll also pay your next 6 months rent. But I'm not promising any more than that. Now get out, and don't come back here again. If I want to talk to you I'll contact you."

Camilla rose and showed Trace to the front door. As they walked along the short passageway she whispered something into his ear. He paused on the doorstep and scribbled a 'phone number onto a slip of paper. Smiling to herself Camilla closed the front door behind Trace and concealed the 'phone number in the hall table drawer. Time, she thought, to go and visit her mother in Wroxborough.

Camilla returned to the lounge to find Elgin deep in thought. "How serious is this?" asked Camilla, suddenly feeling threatened.

"I'm sure we can contain this. Spread some money around. People come cheap you know." This was a veiled reference to the price that Camilla's father had paid for him to marry his rather plain daughter. Nothing so crude as money of course, but an unopposed selection for the constituency seat had set Elgin on the road to the political big time.

"First things first. We have to close Daphne Gibson's big mouth. I guess Davis will have to clock up a few air miles. Then there's the tarts. They'll be cheap enough. Davis will wave his fist under their noses when he pays them off, and that should be enough. But we really have to stop this book in its tracks. Davis again I think. He's good at that sort of thing."

I am fairly meticulous with my research, and as I had identified names that were linked to Elgin I had entered them into a database, along with the dates, the nature of the relationship and other information that I thought might be pertinent. This quickly enabled me to eliminate the business people on Steven Rycroft's list. It still left me with a lot of possibles, even after I had further filtered out the political contacts, local government officials and charity workers.

After double checking the nature of some of the relationships, I eventually came up with a shortlist of a dozen names. I looked at the nature of their businesses, and crossed two names off, as they would have been unlikely to be chasing Government contracts. My final selection included suggestions as to which Government Departments might have been involved, and it was this list that I e-mailed through to Steven Rycroft. Being the TV journalist and personality it was Steven who would do the wining and dining.

CHAPTER NINE

As Marco, real name Mark, waited for the front door to be answered he surveyed the house he was standing in front of. It spoke of money, no doubt about that, but in a restrained way, as though the owners didn't want to attract too much attention to their wealth. The front was quite narrow, but even from the road it was obvious that it extended back a long way. It also stood in a sizeable piece of ground, surrounded by trees. Only the wealthy could afford that sort of privacy.

Tyrone, his buddy from The Zone, the night club they both worked at, had told him about this gig. Some big shot politician owned the house, and his wife had a taste for muscular young men. Tyrone and he fit the bill perfectly, but this was the first time Marco had been invited to this house. Tyrone had also told him that the husband liked to join in sometimes. Marco hoped that today wasn't one of those times. He had nothing against three-somes, as such, but he preferred to choose the other male partner himself. Tyrone and he always worked well together, Marco thought.

The door swung open, and Marco took in the woman that answered. She was dressed in a modest two-piece woollen outfit that probably cost as much as a week of Marco's night club wages. That was OK. So many of these women thought they had to come to the door in their undies, with just a see-through robe on. He preferred the subtle approach. She wasn't an ugly woman, Marco conceded, but she wouldn't win any beauty competitions. Probably about 45, definitely overweight, but not grossly so. Marco hated the really big women. He thought he might have a secret fear of being smothered.

The woman invited him in and introduced herself, then offered him wine, which he declined.

"I'm careful what I put in my body." Marco explained. "Alcohol, drugs, all that sort of thing ruins the muscle tone."

"Pity." Camilla's voice suggested she was genuinely disappointed. "I had a fantasy of you snorting coke off my breasts."

"Oh, I can think of a few things I can do with your breasts, and licking is much better than snorting." Marco leered at Camilla, and she blushed.

Camilla giggled girlishly. "You are so right. I can see we're going to have a wonderful time together." She stood up. "Look, I'll go upstairs and get myself ready. Why don't you have a look around and see if you can find some inspiration. By the way, your money's on the mantelpiece. Come up when you're ready."

She left the room, and Marco quickly crossed to the fireplace to collect his wages. Ten crisp new £20 notes, just as agreed. Satisfied that he wasn't being cheated, he went through to the kitchen and checked out the refrigerator. He found what he was looking for and placed it on the kitchen table. He then made some careful selections from the fruit bowl. Deciding he was now fully equipped to do the job, he went up stairs to find the woman.

Outside a man sat in a car, watching the house from a discrete distance. With the powerful telephoto lens on his camera he never needed to get too close to his subject. He had already taken a few photographs, and was waiting for a chance to take a few more. He saw curtains being drawn across an upstairs window, and decided he probably wouldn't get any more opportunities for a while. He checked his watch. His next appointment was getting close. Deciding to call it a day he drove away from the quiet Wroxborough street.

*　　*　　*

The following day the man was back. This time he was able to get photographs of two men entering the house. The olive skinned Latin type again, and the black guy who had visited the house on other occasions. The men had conveniently stood to one side of the door, which had given him a clear camera shot of the woman as she responded to their arrival. He wasn't surprised to see her wearing a bikini top, with a sarong wrapped around her waste. It was a warm day, no doubt she had been enjoying the sun in her garden.

Impulsively he got out of the car and walked along the street to the neighbouring property. He had seen a car leave the drive just a short while earlier, and there were no signs of life anywhere near the house. He decided to take a chance. He walked through the front gate and slipped around the side of the house. Like the other houses in the street privacy was ensured by lines of tall trees between one garden and the next. Behind the line of trees a wooden fence, about 6 feet high, acted as a more solid barrier. The man worked his way along the fence, looking for some gap or break. At last his patience was rewarded. Behind a small potting shed a fence panel had come loose. It hung towards him. He squeezed himself between the shed and the next fence panel along, and then pressed his face into the gap to see what sort of view he had.

It was better than he could ever have hoped for. He could see between two trees, right across the well manicured lawn to the patio that ran across the rear of the house. Arranged around the patio was a selection of garden furniture, including a couple of full length loungers. It was the occupant, or rather occupants, of one of those loungers that set him reaching for his camera.

The black youth lay outstretched on the lounger. Astride him was the woman, known to him as Camilla Elgin. She was bobbing up and down like a horse rider cantering across a field. On the far side, from the observers' viewpoint, stood the Latin boy, his groin about level with the woman's face. The position of the woman's head left no doubt as to why the boy was positioned there.

The advantage, thought the man, of using a digital camera, is that it makes only the softest of clicks. It doesn't have to make any sort of noise at all, but is designed to reassure the user that the chosen image has been captured. No noisy motor drives were required to move film to the next frame. The man clicked the shutter at frequent intervals, as the three people moved around and changed positions. He made sure he got some really clear shots of the woman's face, zooming the lens until her face filled the frame, along with anything that was close to her face at the time. At last the three people broke for a rest. The woman went inside the house, and laughter floated across the garden to the man's hiding place as the two boys shared a joke. The woman, still naked, returned with a tray of drinks. The man risked a couple more photographs, then eased himself out of his hiding place. He checked his watch to make sure he had plenty of time.

He had already made up his mind what he would do with the photographs. He thought he should check it out with the others, but something told him they wouldn't approve of his idea. No, he decided, he had taken the photos, and so he would take the decision as to what to do with them.

*   *   *

An hour later the News Editor of one of the more downmarket Sunday papers was surprised to receive a very large sized e-mail. Opening it he found it held about 40 files containing digitised photographs. He opened a couple of files at random, more out of curiosity than anything else. He often received photographs this way, sometimes with suggestions for publication, and sometimes they were just someone's idea of a joke. What he saw urged him to open the rest of the files. They were a series of pictures of three people having sex in a garden. They were well taken, and the faces could easily be recognised, if anyone knew who they were. The woman's face was familiar, the News Editor thought, but he couldn't quite place it.

He called over a couple of staff reporters, and asked them if they could identify the woman. They couldn't. Soon bets were being placed on who she was. Word spread around the large, open plan office, and everyone wanted a look at the photos. It was a woman from the gossip column, or Society Page as she preferred it to be called, that collected the kitty. Returning to her desk she interrogated the files and pulled up a photo, which she printed off. Returning to the News Editor's desk she held her photo along side his computer screen for everyone to make the comparison. There was no doubt. The photo, only a month old, was a perfect match for the photo on the screen, providing one ignored what the woman had in her mouth.

The News Editor, a journalist for 30 years, had never said "hold the front page", and nor did he now. He did, however, pull the Managing Editor and two company lawyers out of a very expensive lunch. Sunday's front page, and several inside pages, were sitting in an e-mail on his computer.

The Managing Editor was suspicious about why the photos had been sent. No request for payment had accompanied them, not even a message suggesting they be printed. The e-mail address of the sender didn't help either, as it was an apparently random collection of letters and numbers. No doubt the originator could be traced, thought the Editor, if anyone had the right resources available. On the other hand, he could just treat the e-mail as a gift from God. He decided that God must like him. The lawyers could find no reason not to publish the photos, providing they were suitably doctored in order not to offend public decency, as though that had ever been a priority for this newspaper.

"Publish them" he ordered. "Front page, plus pages 3-7 inclusive. Get one of the juniors to put together a 'who are the men?' piece, as a commentary, The Agony Aunt can give us a couple of hundred words on female mid-life crisis, maybe get a retired MP to do a 'country's going to the dogs' bit, but make sure the words don't get in the way of the pictures." He grinned wolfishly. "I'll see if I can get a quote from our Deputy Prime Minister, but not until the first editions hit the streets. We don't want him spoiling the fun with an injunction. The quote can go into the later editions.

*   *   *

The Deputy Prime Minister was enjoying his after dinner brandy in the company of the other male guests at the dinner party. As tradition demanded, the ladies were in a separate drawing room. Elgin enjoyed these semi formal dinners, where one was invited so that one could be lobbied, but on the other hand one was treated like royalty and the food was usually exceptionally good. A waiter approached his chair. Bending low he whispered into Elgin's ear. Elgin made his apologies and followed the man into the hall.

Elgin was handed a telephone, into which he announced his full title. His jaw dropped as the Managing Editor told him what the front page of his newspaper was showing the next day. He also reminded Elgin that the first copies of his newspaper were already on their way to the all night news stands that served the mainline railway stations. He asked Elgin for a quote.

What Elgin said was totally unprintable for any newspaper that wished to remain on the right side of the Press Complaints Commission. However, the Managing Editor thanked Elgin, and started mentally preparing the short paragraph that would describe Elgin's reaction. Elgin slammed the 'phone down into its cradle, then rushed to the drawing room to summon his wife. His explosive appearance caused quite a stir, but Elgin ignored the protests and questions. Grabbing his wife's arm he dragged her bodily from the room. He hurried her along the hall, until he found a door leading to a small office. He pushed Camilla into the room and shut the door behind them both, turning the key in the lock in order to prevent interruptions.

"What the fuck have you been up to?" Elgin yelled at his wife.

"What do you mean?" stammered Camilla. She had never seen her husband in this state before, and she was frightened.

"You, you stupid slut. You're plastered all over the front pages. You and two young studs. At it like knives, by all accounts"

"I.... I" Camilla was speechless, unable to understand what she was being accused of.

"It must have been last week, when you were in Wroxborough." Elgin's mind raced to try to understand what had happened. "Yes, you and that gigolo Tyrone, and no doubt his pal Marco. The three of you fucking like rabbits in our back garden. Someone got pictures, you stupid cow." His voice had been rising as he worked his way through the puzzle, till now he was shouting again.

Camilla burst into tears, terrified at what she was hearing. Her husband wouldn't be angry about her screwing the two boys, she knew. She had a blank cheque for that, as he had with his women. He must be angry about something else. The key words finally filtered through her terrified brain, *front pages* and *photos*.

"How ….. I don't understand. How did they get them?" she stammered.

"Too late to worry about that now. Its damage limitation. Get your coat, and mine. Call for the car. We can't go back to the flat tonight. It'll be besieged by press by now. We'll go to a hotel while I think about how we deal with this. Oh God." He moaned, holding his head in his hands. "This is a disaster." He unlocked the door and stepped out into the hall. The host, hostess and a small group of the other guests were in a huddle in the middle of the hall, clearly concerned by all the shouting. Elgin put on his brightest political smile, the one normally reserved for the Prime Minister.

"Sorry about that." His voice oozed charm. "Minor crisis. I'm afraid we're going to have to leave now. Urgent Government business, you know. Politicians never get to relax, so it seems." He threw back over his shoulder as Camilla helped him into his coat.

Elgin's dumfounded host showed him to the door, where a car was already waiting for him, summoned over the 'phone by Camilla. They stopped only once, at Kings Cross station to buy a copy of the offending newspaper, before checking into a hotel not far from Russell Square.

Once in their room Elgin dismissed his driver and sat on the bed to think his problems through. He leafed through the pages of the newspaper, trying to assess how bad the damage was. It didn't take long to conclude that the damage couldn't be any worse. He had just read the final word of the very short commentary on the pictures when his mobile 'phone rang. His end of the ensuing conversation was confined to a couple of *yes's* and a *no*. He stabbed at a button to cut the connection.

"Number fucking 10." He spat. "I've to be there at 9 in the morning." He fell silent again, as Camilla perched on an arm chair. She hadn't stopped crying since Elgin's tirade at the dinner party.

Elgin stood up and started pacing the room, slamming his fist into his palm to emphasise his words as he spoke.

"First we've got to get you out of the country. If they start talking to you, you might make matters worse. I'll 'phone British Airways and get you on the first flight out. Not Heathrow though, they'll be watching….. a provincial airport, Birmingham maybe. Then I'll get together with the Press Office at Number 10, we'll draft something for your lawyers to read out. Something along the lines that you're so sorry to have betrayed me, that you will do the right thing and won't oppose a divorce, and of course I'll get custody of the children."

"You're throwing me out?" Camilla could hardly believe her ears.

"Its the only way. You can't stay after something like this, I'd be a laughing stock. This way the PM may just decide not to sack me."

"But all the years I've given to you, all Daddy's money……"

"Daddy's money ran out years ago. You've got very expensive tastes you know." He resisted the temptation to mention her most expensive taste, that for young, well hung gigolos. "We've been living off what I can bring in for years now, and its a good job we haven't had to rely on an MPs salary." He looked at his wife with contempt. Not because of what she had done, but for getting caught doing it. "Don't worry, I'll make sure you don't go hungry. But don't expect to have anything left over for pretty young boys. Maybe you can go on the game and get your sex that way."

Camilla broke down into sobbing again as Elgin leafed through the telephone directory, looking for the number for British Airway's 24 hour booking line. Five minutes later he spoke directly to Camilla again.

"You're on a the 6 am flight to Monastir. Once you get there you can book yourself into a hotel and sit tight until I tell you that its OK to come back. Just don't attract attention to yourself." He started dialling another number on his mobile.

"Damn, Watkins isn't answering his 'phone." He thought for a minute. "I'll ring Knight in Wroxborough. He might be available." Knight obviously was, as Elgin started to issue instructions down the 'phone, about collecting suit cases and packing clothes, and not forgetting Mrs Elgin's passport.

Four hours later Camilla was sat in the back of the limousine that was hired to Elgin whenever he visited Wroxborough, paid for by a grateful constituent (and duly declared in the Register of Member's Interests). Knight, the chauffeur that that Valerie and Clarke had seen in the Wroxborough constituency office, had followed his instructions to the letter. Driving as fast as he dare,

Knight delivered a still tearful Camilla to Birmingham Airport just in time for her flight.

*   *   *

At five minutes to nine Elgin climbed out of his limousine, the door held open by Watkins, and walked the short distance from the car to the door of Number 10 Downing Street. With the exception of a cheery smile and a wave, he ignored the frantic shouts of the press that were gathered across the road waiting for him. The door swung open before he could use the large brass door knocker, and then closed behind him. An hour later he left, again only rewarding the waiting press with a wave. His car whisked him away, the police stopping traffic so he could complete his short journey to the Houses of Parliament.

*   *   *

Elgin had moved from the hotel to his club. His house in Wroxborough and his flat in London were still besieged by the press, so this anonymous Belgravia building was his only refuge. His wife's solicitor had been contacted, and the press release faxed through to him. It would be read out in front of journalists, photographers and TV cameras in front of the Wroxborough house in time to make the Monday morning editions of the papers, but the press, impatient as ever, were still hoping to catch a glimpse of the couple, or to get an unguarded response from someone close to them.

Elgin paced the small bedroom, planning his revenge. His interview with the PM had been acrimonious, but his own attempts at damage limitation had met with approval. As such the PM had said, reluctantly Elgin thought, that he would continue to back Elgin. But the sub text had been clear. No more slip ups.

The photographs, Elgin had no doubt, had something to do with the book that was being written. He couldn't explain why, not even to himself, but he was sure of it. He had one name to work with at present, that of the TV journalist Steven Rycroft. Well, Rycroft would have to bear the brunt of Elgin's revenge for the moment.

CHAPTER TEN

Steven had at last been successful in finding someone to talk to about possible dodgy deals. Through a chain of media contacts he had tracked down a rumour of a major scandal at the Ministry of Defence that had, up till now, been hushed up. Rycroft passed the details on to me and I tried to arrange a meeting with the senior civil servant who would it seemed, know all about it. At first I was dismissed out of hand, and I thought we had hit a brick wall once again, but the following day I received a call suggesting a meeting.

The meeting couldn't be set up any earlier than the following week, but that suited me, as I wanted to go back to Wroxborough first. Twice I had references to someone having died as a result of Elgin's dealings, and this felt like something that I should be following up on. Once again I took the train to the Midlands.

I had struck up something of a relationship with the young receptionist at the local newspaper. After her frosty initial dealings with me she had got used to my appearances, and it took only a cup of coffee and a doughnut to melt her icy exterior. She hadn't worked at the paper for long, she told me after we had exchanged greetings, and I had purchased another the necessary refreshments that now formed the basis of our relationship, so she didn't remember the story I referred to, but she was sure that one of the staff reporters would.

Like most local newspapers it only employed a couple of reporters of its own, relying heavily on amateurs to submit reports of their fetes, football matches and other newsworthy activities, to fill its pages. However, when real news needed reporting the staff reporters were the ones who covered it. Stevie, the receptionist, introduced me to Mike, a shabby 50 year old who had obviously given up any hope of reaching the journalistic heights of a regional newspaper, let alone a national one. I invited him to the pub for a drink, an offer he accepted all too readily.

I told Mike about the local builder who had been badly beaten up, and asked if he knew anything about it. Stevie had found me the right man. Mike had covered the story at the time. Like a good journalist he had kept his notebooks and felt sure he would be able to identify the family for me, after we had finished our drinks. As Mike had finished his I suspected he meant the *next* drinks, so I refilled Mikes glass, and just for good luck filled it again ten minutes later.

Returning to the newspaper office Mike hunted through his piles of old note books until he found the one he was looking for. He flipped through the pages until he found the story.

"Yes," he said. "Its all here." He read through his shorthand for a few minutes, in silence, then he filled me in on what had happened, as he had recorded it at the time. "Best thing you can do is go and see them." He scribbled something on a sheet of paper "That's the name and address. They'll be able to give you it all first hand, I'm sure." In the event he was wrong, but I was still able to get a first hand account.

The Ellis family home, Ellis being the builder's family name, had been bought by a charming old lady, who was clearly only too happy to tell me everything she knew. Over tea and Hobnobs She told me how she had been a family friend of the Ellis's. When Vic Ellis had died so tragically she had bought the house from the family. She took pride in telling me how she had paid well over the odds for the property "just to help them out". No, she didn't have a forwarding address for them, not any more. They had moved to Nottingham, where Violet Ellis had family, apparently.

"You should talk to Billy," she advised me. "Billy would know where the family was."

"And who is Billy," I questioned, gently.

"He was Vic's foreman." She told me. "No, he was more than that. He was Vic's friend from way back when they were school boys together. He only lives along the road. Hang on." She bustled away and returned a moment later with the telephone directory, which she proceeded to search through.

"Here he is." She announced at last. "William Allerdice, but everyone called him Billy, ever since he was knee high. I'll ring him for you."

She bustled off again, and after a few moments I could here her talking to someone over the phone. With a final "OK Billy, I'll tell him." she hung up and returned to the cosy parlour.

"He said he'll meet you in The Journeyman at 6. That's a pub just along the road there, on the corner." She pointed in a general direction westerly direction. "That will give you time for another cup of tea, won't it. Now did I tell you that I once met the Queen?" Oh the joys of being a fake journalist.

*   *   *

Billy Allerdice was a cheerful, stocky fellow, with a weather beaten look that suggested a life spent out doors. He greeted me with a grin, which faded into sadness as I told him what I wanted. He suggested that the story would be better told over a pint of mild, a hint which I took.

"It was a bad business, and no mistake." Stated Billy. "But Vic were always a stubborn man, even as a kid he'd never give into bullies. Earned him a beating or two even back then, but he always came out of top because of it. Earned people's respect, it did, not kow-towing." I let Billy tell the story his own way, having learnt through experience that different people's memories work in different ways. Trying to short circuit their thought processes usually meant that they left out something important.

"Anyway, it sort of came out of the blue, you might say. I was in the yard, in the office, discussing the week's work with him, as usual for a Monday morning, when this bloke came in. Seemed all charm at first. Londoner, he was. Said his name was Scott Davis, even gave us a business card, cheeky bugger. Anyway, he said that he represented various *interests*, and some of these *interests* wanted to go into the building business locally." Billy kept emphasising the word 'interest', almost turning it into a swear word.

"He said there must be plenty of work around, plenty to share, and so why didn't Vic withdraw his tender for the council house maintenance contract, so his *interests* could bid instead. Well Vic said he believed in fair competition, and if his, Davis's *interests* wanted to win the contract all they had to do was come in with the lowest tender, and that was all there was to be said on the subject." Billy paused, to gather his thoughts. I could tell he was starting to get distressed as memories surfaced that were better left buried deep.

"Well, this Davis bloke said Vic was being very stupid, and if he didn't reconsider it would be the worse for him. Vic told him to get out, and if he didn't it would be the worse for Davis. At that Davis left, but said he'd be back. Nothing happened after that, not for a day or so, but they must have been watching the yard. Anyway, it was the Thursday, and Vic was in the yard by himself. It was getting dark, and the yard wasn't well lit. Anyway, Vic locks the office, then starts across the yard to the gate to close that on his way out. He only got half way when he was set on. Two of them, he said, when he could speak again. They had baseball bats, or something of the like, and they beat poor Vic senseless. He wasn't found for two hours, when Violet sent their lad, Charlie, round to the yard to look for him." He took a big gulp of his pint of mild, emptying the pot. I signalled to the barman, to indicate that he should refill the glass.

"Vic was in hospital for three weeks, then on crutches for nearly three months. He was a broken man. Oh, his injuries healed, but the beating had knocked all the stuffing out of him. I was bugger-all use to him. Without him to tell me what to do I wasn't able to keep the business going, and it went bust. It was all sold off to pay the bills, but there was a little bit left for Vic and his family, but Vic could never work again, and that broke his heart. He was a proud man, didn't want to take money from the state, and to live on benefits really hurt him. I think he died of a broken heart in the end." Billy sipped slowly at his beer, clearly struggling to hold back the tears. Men like Billy don't cry in public.

"The police investigated, of course, but they never got anyone for it. That Davis character had a rock solid alibi. He was in London, with a dozen witnesses to back him up. No one had actually seen the two men who did the attack, no one saw them arrive or leave, no one saw a car even, so it was like trying to find ghosts. After a while all the police could do was put the file in a drawer, and when Vic died they lost interest altogether."

"What happened to Vic's family?" I kept my voice so low it was almost a whisper. Billy straightened, overcoming his grief.

"Oh, Violet took them off to Nottingham. She had come from there, and still had family. She did all right out of the sale of their house, enough to live on if she was careful. My wife kept in contact. They'd been friends ever since Vic and Violet got married. Violet died a couple of years back, and then we lost touch with the rest of the family."

"The rest?" I asked.

"Yes, Charlie, I've already mentioned, but there was a daughter too, Valerie. She was a bit older." Valerie? A coincidence, I wondered. "I was Godfather to them both, and my Enid was Godmother. Pity we've lost touch."

"You don't happen to know what happened to Valerie, do you?" I asked.

"I think she went off to London to work after her Mum died. She was quite a looker, I can tell you, brainy too. She'll do all right, I'm sure. Charlie must be doing well. I saw him a couple of weeks ago, looking very prosperous." He sipped at his beer again. "I've got a photo at home, taken not long before Vic was attacked. Tell you what, "he emptied his pint pot again, "you fill that up, and I'll nip home and get it."

He was gone only five minutes. When Billy returned he had a large silver picture frame in his hand. Clearly the photograph was a prized possession. He handed the frame to me. The photograph showed a middle aged man and woman, obviously Vic and Violet, and two younger people. There was a boy of about 11 or 12, and a teenage girl. I looked closer. In the dim light it wasn't easy to be certain, but I was sure that I was looking at a 10 year old picture of Steven Rycroft's PA. She was using the surname of Mayfield now though, if it was her.

"Does the name Mayfield mean anything to you, Billy?" I asked, as casually as I could.

"Oh, yes, but I haven't heard that name in years. It was Violet's maiden name." Bingo!

"Another pint Billy? Or maybe a short?" I asked, handing the photo frame back to him.

*   *   *

I travelled back to London, tapping notes into my laptop as we headed South at 100 miles an hour. My discoveries of the day would make a good chapter for the book. My mobile chirped into life. Steven Rycroft's name appeared in the little screen.

"High Steven," I greeted him, cheerfully.

"Where are you." He sounded agitated.

I told him I was on the train, but I was expecting to arrive in London with the next quarter of an hour.

"Look, can you get yourself over here. There's been a development." He wouldn't say any more, but I could tell from Steven's voice it wasn't good news.

Less than an hour later I stepped out of a taxi in Steven's street. The driver couldn't get close to the house because of the police cars that were filling the roadway. I brushed past a motorcyclist who was fiddling with the engine of her bike, and apologised absent mindedly. As I reached the front door the police were just leaving. Steven called me in.

I entered the house to be greeted by a scene of utter devastation. The furniture was all smashed, faeces was smeared over the wall, books were scattered and torn, pictures torn from their frames, and the frames themselves shattered.

"Its like this upstairs too. The only thing that's been stolen are the computers, mine and Valerie's."

"Valerie? Where …." Steven interrupted the question.

"Not here, I'm relieved to say. I'd sent her to Metro to pick up some documents for me. I went to meet Sam, to hand over the latest chapter, and the place was like this when I got back."

"Coincidence? Or have we struck a nerve?"

"Oh, we've struck a nerve alright. Look at this." He handed me the front page of a newspaper. "I found it pinned to the door of the office. I took it down before the police arrived. I don't want them interfering."

The newspaper was The Wroxborough Dispatch, the newspaper whose offices I had been in that very day. The headline hit me between the eyes with the impact of a bullet fired from close range.

"EX-COUNCILLOR DIES IN PORTUGAL ROAD ACCIDENT"

I noted with some irony that the by-line was Mike's, my new found friend on the Wroxborough local paper. I read on to confirm my worst fears. Daphne Gibson had died when her car had plunged off the road near her villa in Portugal, out of control, and apparently suffering from brake failure. The fact that the newspaper story had been left in such a prominent position could only be interpreted as a warning that Steven could suffer a similar accident. With what I had found out today I knew that the threat wasn't an idle one.

"I think you were right not to show the police. They might think you had something to do with Daphne Gibson's death." Which you did indirectly, I didn't say out loud, as did I. "and we don't want them to make that sort of connection. How do you think they found out about you're involvement in the book?" I wondered aloud.

"I guess I must have been followed here. Remember, Davis knows Sam. It wouldn't be difficult to keep an eye on her, see who she met, then follow them until they'd been checked out. When they checked me out they obviously came up with Metro TV, added two and two together and came up with the right answer. Did you see the Sunday papers"

"Camilla Elgin? Yes, I saw them. Who did that do you think? Is it connected to this?"

"As for who did it, I can't be sure. I have my suspicions, but I'm afraid I can't share them with you. There is someone who would be in great danger if they were discovered. More danger than I realised, perhaps. Is this connected to the Camilla Elgin story? I think it would be too much of a coincidence to be anything else."

"So, what do we do now?"

"I've already told Valerie to keep clear of here. Its possible that Elgin's organisation doesn't know about her yet. We'll try not to meet here in future. I'll move into the cottage. Its in Gustav's name, not in mine, so there's no reason to suppose its known about. We'll keep in contact by e-mail and 'phone. If we have to meet we'll do it elsewhere."

A thought struck me, and I wandered across to the window. A crack ran down the length of it, but it didn't obscure my view along the road. The motorcyclist was still tinkering with her bike. I called Steven across. "Do you know her?"

"I don't think so. I don't know anyone in the street who owns a motorbike. It isn't a motorbike sort of neighbourhood, really."

"Its a good way of following someone around London." I commented.

"Call yourself a taxi. When you leave I'll watch. If she leaves as well I'll ring your mobile."

In the ten minutes it took for the taxi to arrive I told Steven about my trip to Wroxborough, leaving out only my knowledge of Valerie's real identity, and the photo I had seen that revealed it. If Steven wanted to keep secrets I saw no reason why I shouldn't as well. I had a feeling that Steven already knew this story. I would have expected more questions seeking clarification of some of the details, and they weren't forthcoming.

The taxi had only just turned the corner into the Fulham Road when my mobile bleeped to indicate a text message had arrived. I read it quickly. It was short and sweet. "You've grown a tail."

I sneaked a glance through the back window of the cab. Sure enough, two cars back was the motorcyclist. The girl's long hair billowed from under the rim of her crash helmet.

I had told the driver to take me to Islington, which was close enough to home without having to be specific. I didn't want the motorcyclist to get too much information for free. Now I tapped on the partition and re-directed him to Oxford Circus. He dropped me outside the underground station. I had read lots of spy books in my youth, and always wondered if I could outwit someone following me.

If the girl wanted to follow me she would first have to find somewhere to leave her motorbike. By that time I would already be on the underground platform. I took a Victoria line train to Green

Park. Above me on the pavement of Oxford Street, the girl gabbled an explanation into her mobile 'phone, seeking instructions. Finding herself defeated, at least temporarily, she rode off.

At Green Park I made my way through the tunnels to the Piccadilly Line platforms. I got on the train, but kept close to the doors. As they started to slide shut I stepped back out onto the platform, narrowly avoiding the doors closing on my coat and trapping it. The platform was empty now, and with nowhere for a person to conceal themselves I felt sure that I had avoided being followed this far, or if not my "tail" was now speeding northwards at 30 m.p.h. I took the next train and changed trains again at Kings Cross, joining the Northern Line, finally resurfacing into the cool night air at Angel station. I made my way to my flat.

I ignored the protests of my cat as I handed it over to Lilly. She seemed unsurprised that I was off on another journey. I told her I was going to Hong Kong, and she said "that's nice" as though I had announced a day trip to Clacton. I packed a small suitcase with the few things I would need, picked up my laptop once again, and headed out of my flat for an extended absence. I was sure that no one had identified me, but I didn't want to take any risks. Thirty minutes later I booked into the Holiday Inn Express on Old Street. This, I decided, would be my home for the foreseeable future. Pity I haven't got longer foresight.

I had, indirectly, been responsible for the death of Daphne Gibson. Whatever she may have been at one time all I had seen when I went to Portugal was a sad, lonely old woman, who regretted her past and wanted to make amends. Now she was dead, and I might as well have committed the murder myself. I was absolutely certain it was murder. I had seen her car parked next to her house, and it was almost brand new. The likelihood of genuine brake failure was minimal. I drank myself into oblivion thinking that through. It didn't help, and it gave me a stinking hangover. I spent the next few days typing up the draft of my chapter on Vic Ellis, wondering whose death I might cause with that.

*   *   *

Camilla Elgin was feeling vengeful. In her hotel in a Tunisian holiday resort she had all that she needed, and certainly all that her credit cards could provide. The young waiters had learnt to avoid going near her room, she noticed, and it was the older or uglier ones that responded to her requests for room service now. She was bored, and had plenty of time on her hands to plot her revenge on her ungrateful husband. Spite gnawed away at her like a dog chewing a bone.

Over a thousand miles away, the News Editor who had received the revealing photographs of her received another unexpected e-mail. It simply said that Camilla Elgin had caught a flight to Monastir. A reporter and a photographer were ordered to go home, pack their bags and get on the next available flight to Tunisia.

CHAPTER ELEVEN

"Who is this bloke?" Elgin was sat in The Grapes with Scott Davis.

"No idea yet, Boss." Davis made the comment suggest that it wasn't his fault for not knowing. "He might not even be connected to this in any way."

"He arrived right after you trashed Rycroft's place, and Rycroft seemed to be expecting him. That makes him connected. If he wasn't Rycroft would have got rid of him. You don't entertain guests after your house has been ransacked." Elgin mused for a moment. "And it looks like he deliberately gave your girl Tracy the slip. That means he not only knew he was being followed, but was actually expecting it. She said he told the cab driver to take him to Islington?"

"That's what she thought, Boss, but she was a few yards away."

"OK, Islington sounds nothing like Oxford Circus, so I'm guessing she heard right. Also you don't have to go through Oxford Circus to get to Islington from Fulham, there's much quicker ways, especially at that time of day. No, he definitely gave her the slip deliberately, which makes him connected to both Rycroft and the book."

"What do you want me to do?"

"Keep on it. Keep Rycroft under observation, that goes without saying, but make sure that if the mystery man turns up again you're able to follow him, and in a way that makes it impossible for him to get away next time."

"I'll get Tracy to take her brother Gareth along. He can ride pillion, and if the mystery man pulls any more stunts like that Gareth can follow on foot. We're having a bit of trouble with Rycroft as well though. He's no longer at the Fulham gaff, and the closest we can get to him is when he leaves work. He takes a taxi to the underground car park at Hyde Park, the one on Park Lane, but we can't identify him when he comes out. We've not been lucky enough to pick him out once he's in his car, and we can't risk showing out by getting too close. There isn't really anywhere near the exit where someone can hang about without being noticed.".

In fact Rycroft wasn't using a car. He was entering through one pedestrian entrance and leaving by another, before taking a taxi to Marylebone Station and a train to Banbury.

"You'll have to get to him through the other guy then. We know where Rycroft works so we can latch onto him again any time we want. What's this Gareth like? Is he sound?"

"I wouldn't trust him in an empty room that's already been burgled, but he won't double cross us. He knows what he'd get from me if he did."

"OK, make it happen. But make sure he doesn't know I'm involved. What does Tracy think is going on?"

"The usual. Bit of private detective work, errant husband, that sort of style."

"OK, keep it like that. Buy her something nice out of petty cash. She led us to Rycroft, which was all we really asked her to do."

"And me?"

"You know the deal. Yours will be in your bank account tomorrow."

"That reminds me, my cuckoo clock needs repairing. I better go and see my clock maker soon." Davis grinned and left the pub. Elgin drained his glass, and went to the gents so as to leave a sufficient gap for Davis and himself not to be seen together outside the pub.

*   *   *

Tracy had followed her instructions and positioned herself outside Metro TV's South Bank office block, and now sat sideways on the seat of her motorbike, her brother Gareth at her side. They both wore tabards suggesting they were among the many motorcycle couriers that plied their trade around the commercial centres of Britain's capital city. They made desultory conversation, trying to avoid mentioning Scott Davis's name. Gareth hated the man with all his heart, but was equally scared of him. He glanced sideways at his sister to remind himself of what Davis had done to her the night before. The bruise had lost some of its fierceness now, but was still clearly visible, mimicking the shape of Davis's gold sovereign ring. She had got that just because she had forgotten to pick up Davis's dry cleaning, but Gareth suspected it was really because she had lost track of the mystery man that had been at Rycroft's house.

Elgin may have forgiven Tracy for losing the mystery man, but Davis hadn't. The petty cash box at Get Real Communications was £100 lighter, but Tracy would never see what had been purchased with it.

The name Elgin meant little to Tracy and nothing to Gareth. Tracy knew that Elgin owned the company that employed her, but had never met the man. Gareth didn't even know that much. Shown a picture of the Deputy Prime Minister of his country Gareth would probably ask which Football Club he managed.

Tracy straightened up and turned to straddle her bike. Her brother needed no urging to scramble on behind her. He looked across and recognised the man they had been following for the last few days, emerging from the imposing front of the office block and crossed the pavement to board the taxi that was waiting for his arrival.

Tracy and Gareth's hearing was muffled by their crash helmets, even if they hadn't been too far away to hear where Rycroft told the driver to take him, but Tracy wasn't worried about that. In a race through London against a taxi Tracy knew there could be only one winner. In fact in a race through London with any four wheeled vehicle there could only be one winner.

The journey wasn't a long one. Just as far as the Royal Festival Hall. After paying the cab Rycroft disappeared inside, Gareth as close behind as he could be without attracting attention.

Gareth returned half an hour later. "Do you know how much they charge for a cup of coffee?" he whined.

"Never mind that. Who did he meet?" snapped Tracy.

"Oh, yeah. He went into the caff and met that bloke over there." Gareth pointed.

Tracy recognised the man who had given her the slip a few days before, standing waiting for a free taxi to pass. He was in luck as a vehicle did a U turn to pull over on his side of the road.

"Ok, we're going to stick with him. Get on!" she commanded.

*   *   *

Finally attracting the attention of a taxi, I climbed into the back and settled down for the ride. It would be a long one, I decided. I had told the driver to take me to Regents Park Zoo, which he would. A walk round the zoo for a couple of hours, then perhaps an even longer walk in Hyde Park. I needed the exercise anyway. That, of course, would involve another taxi tide through London's traffic clogged streets. Dinner somewhere expensive, I thought, while my tail waited outside and watched me eat, then perhaps a stroll along The Embankment before retiring to the hotel that I had booked into on Rycroft's instructions.

Tomorrow I would give them the slip again.

Rycroft had spotted them easily enough that morning. How they thought they could get away with using the same girl twice he couldn't fathom. Obviously Davis wasn't that bright, or there was only a limited supply of people he trusted to do his foot slogging for him. The pimply teenager was a new variation, of course, but it didn't take a genius to work out why he was there. He had stood out in the café of the Royal Festival hall like a giraffe on an iceberg, in his jeans and hoody, with a tabard over the top and a crash helmet tucked under his arm. He didn't look too bright either, but that feeling would be tested the following day.

It had been unlucky that they had caught up with me again, but it was to be expected. Now I had to lose them again so I could get on with my work without their interference. It meant that Rycroft and I couldn't meet in London any more. Once I lost them again they would be all over him like a rash, but we would be OK keeping in touch by 'phone and e-mail. We had already agreed that Valerie mustn't be put in any danger, so she couldn't meet me either.

*   *   *

Giving the boy the slip the next day wasn't as easy as I had imagined it would be. He may not have been very bright, but he was cunning. He stayed on the underground platform right until the last moment before the doors shut, then stepped aboard. Being as thin as a whippet helped as the doors slid shut.

I tried not to look at him, though he was in clear sight in the next carriage, but as each station came and went I saw him move himself close to the door as the train slowed to a halt. If I stepped off the train at the last moment so could he. I changed trains a couple of times, but in the manner of a normal person, rather than the manner of an ultra paranoid secret agent.

At last my chance came. At Hammersmith, travelling West on the District Line, a young woman boarded the train weighed down with bags, an occupied baby buggy and a set of three other stepping stone children, all girls. I smiled at her with sympathy, but she only managed a scowl in return. Three stops further along, at Turnham Green, I saw her make her preparations to leave the train, expertly corralling the children, picking up her various bags and pushing the buggy to the centre of the doorway. The child in the buggy turned its head to smile up at its mother. She made cooing noises in return.

The train pulled to a stop, and as the doors slid open I stepped forward. "Here, let me help." I turned the words into action by picking up the smallest child, hardly big enough to be out of a baby buggy itself, and lowered her to the platform. I then half stepped down myself, apparently assisting the next oldest child. The girl dodged my grasp, as I guessed she might. She had clung, limpet like, to her mother during the short journey, and I could see she didn't like being amongst strangers.

From the corner of my eye I checked what the pimply youth was doing. He was still standing near the door, but was relaxed, unconcerned that my act of altruism was anything other than it seemed. I lunged for the child, forcing me to lean further from the train as I apparently overbalanced. The child once again evaded my hands and made its own way to the safety of its mother's side. The final sibling stepped onto the platform from behind me.

I straightened up and turned as if to get back on the train, just as the door alarm started its high pitched warble.

I was halfway through the doors as they started to slide shut, and all I had to do was take a step back, which I did. Gareth slammed himself against the closing doors of his carriage, but it was already too late. I watched his face collapse in despair as the train started to accelerate past me. I couldn't resist raising my hand to give him a little farewell wave.

His look turned from despair to shock, and that was the last I saw of him. I turned and followed my unwitting accomplices up the stairs and crossed to another platform.

*   *   *

"He knew you were following him!" Davis screamed into Gareth's terrified face.

"He must have done." Whimpered Gareth. "All he did was ride around on the tube, getting on and off trains. Then he waved at me."

"Oh, very fucking friendly, I'm sure" Davis released his grip and allowed Gareth to sink into a worn out armchair.

"When do you think he spotted you?" he asked Tracy, keeping his tone level. She was cowering on the settee, trying to make herself as invisible as possible. She knew Davis of old, and dreaded what might happen next.

"He must have known all along. All that stuff with the zoo, and Hyde Park, then Langhams. He was stringing us along, probably thought he was teaching us a lesson."

"OK, that means that he either spotted you when he came out of the Festival Hall, or Rycroft had already spotted you and warned him." He took two steps towards Tracy and loomed over her. Tracy tried to shrink herself into the very fabric of her settee. "You did just what we agreed?"

"Of course. Stayed further back, didn't park too close to his office, wore the tabard so I would look like the other bikers."

"So what went wrong?"

"I don't know. But I told you it wouldn't work. I told you he was wise….." her words were stopped by the arrival of Davis's fist. She crashed sideways to sprawl along the sofa, her injured face screened now by her arms as she tried to ward off further blows. Davis rarely stopped at one punch.

"Less of your lip, you fucking stupid tart."

"You leave her alone. You don't fucking touch her." Gareth spurred into action in defence of his injured sister. Davis anticipated his approach and swung round, landing a back handed blow that sent the boy reeling back to his chair, slumping down, too dazed to move.

"You two make me fucking sick, you really do. I don't know why I put up with you." A couple of things sprang to Tracy's mind, but she was too cowed to say anything more.

"You two better hope we don't lose our jobs over this. I'm off to the pub." With which he stormed out of the shabby sitting room, leaving the injured woman and her brother to their misery.

*   *   *

Timothy Elgin wasn't the sort of person to leave things to chance. He knew that the woman Tracy was likely to give herself away again. She wasn't trained for what she had been doing, and so had to rely on the people she followed not suspecting that anyone would want to follow them. Rycroft knew he was being followed, as did the unknown stranger, and so would still be looking out for anything unusual. Happily, for Elgin, he was a man of immense power and considerable influence.

He read the report that he had just received, which confirmed much of what he knew already from Scott Davis and his woman. However, where their trail went cold at Turnham Green Underground Station, this report continued in some detail. The man had caught another train back towards the city, changed at Monument, took the escalator connection to Bank and eventually emerged into the daylight at Old Street Station. It wasn't difficult, as he no longer suspected he was being followed, to watch him as far as his current residence, the Old Street Holiday Inn Express.

From that point it was a matter of some skilful questioning assisted by the timely distribution of £20 notes. The mystery man was Clarke Nevis, a novelist who had recently published a somewhat controversial book. The report had a photo of Clarke attached to it, lifted straight from the back cover of the book.

Elgin realised that if he had seen the man for himself he would have recognised him instantly. The man had sat opposite him in his constituency office and quizzed him about his life. He also realised that the penalty for employing someone like Davis was that he had probably never read a book in his life, or he would have recognised the man for himself. The only way Davis would have known the man's name would be if it had appeared on page 3 of the more down market newspapers. The same seems to have applied to the woman, Tracy, and her brother.

Elgin made a mental note to make sure Davis used the digital cameras that had been so expensively bought for the company. Why Davis hadn't loaned one to Tracy Elgin couldn't imagine.

The report continued, giving Nevis's real address, his e-mail address, and the 'phone numbers of both his landline and mobile.

Elgin scribbled a note of thanks and asked the originator of the report to keep up observation of both Rycroft and Nevis. He used the words "grave National importance" to justify his request, and sent the message by hand.

*   *   *

The recipient of the note grunted when he read what had been said. He had undertaken the surveillance as a personal favour more than anything, and on the understanding that it was a "one off". Now he was being asked to continue it.

Surveillance operations cost money, and his limited budget didn't extend to favours such as this. Not only that, he had pulled a team of 6 highly skilled operatives off a long standing observation of a man with some very interesting connections in both Iran and Afghanistan. How the surveillance of a reputable journalist and a popular novelist could rank as being of "grave National importance" he couldn't fathom, but he had no intention of expending another penny on it until he had some idea of why he was doing it. If there was no good reason, his staff would be back doing their proper jobs within minutes.

The man had considerable power and influence himself, and now he used a little of it. He lifted his 'phone and dialled a number. He didn't bother to introduce himself before speaking. "Send me up Timothy Elgin's file will you".

*   *   *

Five hours later the man trashed his third attempt at an e-mail in reply to Timothy Elgin. Elgin wasn't a man to upset lightly, and so every word he wrote had to be chosen with the utmost care. It mustn't sound like a refusal to help. It must sound like he had the deepest desire to help, but was hamstrung and unable to do so.

At last he found words he was happy with. He looked at his watch, which told him he was already late for dinner with his beautiful wife and the daughter they doted on. He would ring and apologise while he travelled. Timothy Elgin was no longer a concern of his, and an outstanding debt had been paid with interest.

*   *   *

Timothy Elgin was, to say the least, unhappy. It was the next day and he was reading the e-mail that had been addressed to his most private mailbox, the one even his closest aids couldn't access.

To say Elgin was furious was an understatement. His "grave National importance" had been trumped with "limited resources" and "competing priorities". If he wished to make a formal request for the operation to continue, then of course the department would be more than happy to place its resources at his, Elgin's, disposal but otherwise "…… I'm sure you will understand when I say my hands are tied."

Pompous little shit, thought Elgin. Well he'd get his when the next review of his departmental expenditure came round. See how he liked half his department being cut, and his own job with it.

So, what to do now? Going after Nevis seemed like the most sensible answer, but was loaded with risk. Without knowing what Nevis had, and who else had it, he could make matters worse. No, this was a time for subtlety. With that in mind Elgin wished he didn't have to use a blunt instrument like Davis, but needs must, etc.

*   *   *

Like many people, I find the food served in certain types of British hotel completely uneatable. However, I was blessed by the location of Old Street, which is not too far from the curry capital of the UK, Brick Lane. I had a favourite restaurant and ate there most nights since I had been staying in the hotel, working my way steadily through the menu. I had yet to be disappointed with my choices.

I wasn't surprised to find my hotel room had been burgled when I returned to it on this particular night, smelling slightly of cumin and garlic. We had led Elgin's stooges a merry dance, but it was too much to hope that we had fooled them completely. This confirmed it.

Were we supposed to see the girl and her gormless side kick? Were they there to provide a distraction while real professionals kept back at a safe distance, seeing without being seen? The theft from my room seemed to confirm this thought.

There was only one item missing. My expensive iPod still lay on the bed side table, as did a heap of small change. My travelling grip had been ransacked, but nothing taken from it. A professional thief would have had the lot, then sorted the wheat from the chaff later, somewhere safe from premature discovery. The only item missing was my laptop. I laughed out loud, then 'phoned Steven. As I did so I pulled my key ring out of my pocket, just to reassure myself. Yes, the memory stick was still firmly attached.

*   *   *

"Have you tried to start it up?" Elgin asked Davis.

"No, Boss. You said not to."

"Good. Now, lets see what we've got." Elgin raised the lid of the laptop and pressed the "start" button. The computer went through its start up sequence, then stopped, a dialogue box on the screen requesting a password.

"We have to be careful here, Boss. Some computers are rigged so if you put the wrong password in three times it will lock you out completely."

"I'm not a complete fool, Davis. I know that. It's no surprise that he's password protected it though. So what do you think he would use?"

"Mother's maiden name? The title of one of his books? How about his cat's name?"

Unbeknown to Nevis, Davis had visited the Islington apartment block and spoken to Lilly.

Elgin thought for a moment. "He hasn't any children and he isn't married, so those sots of names are ruled out. Also he's not stupid enough to use *password* or *123456* or anything like that. I read somewhere that pet's names are one of the most commonly used passwords. OK, I'll go with that for the first attempt." Elgin carefully typed in the word "Alice".

It is true that its possible to make a computer lock itself if the wrong password is entered three times. Its also possible to make it do that after the first incorrect attempt. It's also possible to make it wipe itself clean of all files after the first wrong attempt. Nevis had paid an old friend a lot of money to make sure his computer did exactly that. He had also paid him to make the display screen show the words "The real password was 'Camilla'" before it shut itself down completely and irrevocably.

Elgin swore long and loudly in his frustration, drawing alarmed looks from the other customers in The Grapes. The irony of the choice of name to use as a password was completely lost on him.

Elgin would have to completely re-load the operating system just to make the laptop usable again, and if he did he would find nothing of interest left on the computer. A team of forensic computer specialists might stand a chance of resurrecting the original files, but to go to someone like that Elgin would have to take the risk of them reading the files' contents, and he couldn't have anyone but himself doing that.

OK, he thought. Time to take a more direct approach with Mr fucking Nevis.

CHAPTER TWELVE

I'm not the sharpest tool in the box, by a big margin, but neither am I the dullest. We had rattled Elgin's cage in a big way, and he had started to show his teeth. First the trashing of Rycroft's Fulham house, then the theft of my laptop. I smiled inwardly to myself again about that one. Oh to be a fly on the wall when he had seen that last message appear on the laptop's screen.

I was now starting to feel a little nervous. All the evidence we had so far suggested that Davis was a nasty piece of work, and Elgin wasn't at all afraid to use him as a blunt instrument if need be. Time for me to move lodgings again, at the very least.

The worst part was not knowing what Davis looked like. I could walk past him a dozen times a day and not know it.

Valerie offered me floor space at her place, but much as I was tempted I had to reluctantly refuse. To the best of our knowledge Elgin didn't yet know about Valerie, which firstly kept her safe, and secondly meant she could carry on working on the project without attracting attention.

My new hotel was one of those at the top end of Tottenham Court Road. More expensive, but also a less likely place for Davis to try anything if he located me. I moved in the dead of night, when it would be easy to spot anyone following me. Old Street had been empty as I left the hotel, not even a parked car. The taxi had made the journey along City Road, and past Kings Cross without a single vehicle passing in either direction. I didn't regard the night buses or the police cars as a serious threat. It wasn't until we reached the Kings Cross area that traffic started to pick up. Unless Elgin had the use of a helicopter equipped with infra red tracking equipment I was as sure as I could be that I hadn't been followed.

The next day I replaced my laptop, off the shelf from PC World, then took it along to my old University friend to have it booby trapped again. If he was curious he hid it well, and we agreed to meet up for a drink when time allowed. I was sure he would pursue the arrangement, just to try to find out what I was up to.

Steven, Valerie and I were working mainly through 'phone contact now. Steven was busy recording a new series of documentaries about government waste, so Valerie and I were doing most of the actual research. Valerie didn't have a good internet access from her flat, and so worked most of the day from a friend's place. I hadn't plucked up the courage to try to find out if it was a male or female friend, and she wasn't saying. In the meantime I continued to churn out draft chapters for the book.

They weren't very good, I would have been the first to admit. Then again they didn't have to be. They had to be convincing, which they were. Well they were up to a point. I still needed a smoking gun.

I rang Steven to make sure he would be next to his fax machine at a certain time, then went off to meet Sam Walker to deliver the next draft.

I had agreed to meet Sam in a Prèt â Manger on Oxford Street. As I crossed Tottenham Court Road into Oxford Street I slowed down and took care to look around me. I spotted the pimply youth almost at once, standing directly opposite the coffee shop. He had a livid bruise on his face, which even his hoody couldn't conceal. The boy's presence meant they had followed Sam to the meet. I crossed the road, so that I was on the same side as the boy, then turned to look through the window of Waterstones, apparently absorbed in the latest book releases. I even had time to recognise the fact that my own effort was still on display.

Using the shop window as a mirror I tried to make out where the girl might be. Not far from her motorbike, I knew. I saw the bike, parked up by the curb at the entrance to Rathbone Place. Could the girl be inside the coffee shop, I wondered?

Wherever she was I had to get out of the area without attracting attention. The youth was intent on watching the people entering and leaving Prèt â Manger, giving me the chance to step sideways into the entrance of Waterstones. I found a quiet book lined alcove and keyed a text into my mobile. Following the burgling of my hotel room I was now using an unregistered pay-as-you-go. I asked Sam to take her time finishing her coffee, then make her way back to work. I suggested a trip to the Virgin Megastore as a justification for her journey from Faringdon Road.

I moved into a more open part of the shop, from where I could see across the road. While I browsed the book displays Sam finished her coffee, taking a further 10 minutes to do it. I watched as she left the coffee shop and turned right towards the nearby record shop. The girl motorcyclist came out behind her, and made a hand signal that clearly instructed the boy to follow Sam. The girl herself returned to her bike, where she waited to see what would happen next.

Her 'phone obviously rang, presumably the boy giving a progress report. After about 15 minutes Sam returned along Oxford Street carrying a Virgin carrier bag and heading for Tottenham Court Road Underground Station. The boy followed on foot while the girl started her motorbike and followed at as slow a pace as she could manage without falling off the bike. Only when Sam had clearly entered the underground station did she speed up, heading towards Holborn, following the same track as the Central Line beneath her feet.

I waited another 10 minutes, actually finding a book I wanted to buy, and then left my hiding place. To avoid being spotted by the girl motorcyclist, if she doubled back, I cut along Rathbone Place, heading through the back streets to Russell Square.

*   *   *

"He's staying at that hotel." Davis passed a slip of paper across the table to Elgin. They were tucked away in a rear booth in the corner of The Grapes, once again.

Elgin picked it the paper and shook a drip of lager from the corner, a look of distaste distorting his mouth.

"You're sure he didn't see you?"

"No way Boss. He didn't even look back, didn't pause, didn't stop to tie his shoe lace, nothing. I had him in my eye from the moment he crossed Tottenham Court Road into Oxford Street. He spotted the boy, Gareth, alright, and did a crafty sidestep into a book shop, but I could see the door, and when he left I just went back into Rathbone Place a little. As soon as I could see he was coming my way I just ducked into the entrance of that big Royal Mail place, had a chat with the doorkeeper until Nevis walked past, then back into the street and Bob's you Auntie's husband."

Elgin ignored Davis's bragging, deep in thought about what to do next. Mr Nevis needed eliminating, but he wasn't sure if it could be achieved without leaving a trail that led back to him. Davis was expendable, and had to too much to lose on his own account to talk. A bit of string pulling here and there could make sure he got off if he was caught, providing there was no hard evidence to link him to the crime.

Davis had done that sort of thing before. A couple of thugs, kept at arms length, would do the actual job. Providing they weren't found there was no case against Davis. If they were found, and they talked, then it would be a conspiracy charge, and they were damned difficult to prove. No, Davis would be OK.

The real danger was Rycroft. How would he react to Nevis going missing? Would he go to the police? Would he go underground and continue his campaign? If Nevis went then Rycroft had to go too, along with all the evidence. After that all there was left were a few badly written drafts of a work of fiction. People might talk, but talking didn't hurt. It was what people could prove that put you in the dock.

Elgin realised he needed advice before he decided what to do next. He was too close to this. The idea of taking advice from Davis was ludicrous, so it had to be Otto and Elsa.

"OK, stake out the hotel" Elgin loved gangster talk, "see where he goes, who he sees, but stay clear. No physical contact, OK?"

"You're the boss, Boss. It would be easier if I was staying in the hotel, of course. Hanging around the lobby attracts attention if you're not a guest." He let the suggestion hang in the air.

"Do what you have to. Just make sure you identify anyone he meets, inside the hotel and out."

*　　　*　　　*

Otto Langsdorf detested London, and he detested Timothy Elgin summoning him to the city even more. The fact that he and his sister were being wined and dined in one of the city's finest hotels, in the restaurant founded by one of the elite celebrity chefs, was a small consolation. At least Elgin had the sense to book them a private dining room.

"Are you sure that Rycroft and Nevis are on their own in this?" Langsdorf asked.

"As far as we can work it out. We've seen no sign of anyone else."

"Hmm. I'm not so sure." Elsa Peters interjected. " The night the party took place at Trace's house Rycroft was hosting a live debate on TV. He couldn't have taken that video footage as well."

"Nevis could have done that by himself. I know he was in Wroxborough because of that fucking interview I gave him. That was your doing." Elgin glared at Elsa Peters.

"Oh shit." Peters gasped. "There was a woman with him. The day of the interview he had some woman along. Said she was his personal assistant. Bloody hell, what was her name?" Peters pressed her hands against the sides of her head as though to physically squeeze the name of the female visitor from her memory.

"I remember now. Pretty thing, around 28, 29 or so. He did say her name but it didn't register with me." Elgin recalled.

"Doesn't matter anyway. Nevis didn't use his real name. I can't remember what name he did use, but it'll be in the office diary. It wasn't Nevis anyway. If he used a false name then she probably did as well. Pity we don't have CCTV in the office. The interview was set up using Metro TV's name. If she has anything to do with them someone would recognise a picture if we had one to show around."

"Too late now, anyway." Langsdorf concluded. "What it does mean is that there's at least one more player on their team, and we have no idea who she is, or what she has to do with us. Why is Rycroft so interested in you anyway, Tim?"

"I've been trying to work that out. He's one of the reptiles, of course, even if he is TV. That might be all there is to it. Just a glory seeking newshound looking for a scoop, but I don't think so. I knew him at University, slightly, but we never had any real dealings. He wasn't in the same crowd as I hung out with."

Otto knew that crowd. Hard playing, hard drinking semi-thugs for the most part. No wonder so many of them had ended up in politics.

"What about Nevis?"

"No contact with him, ever, before now. I think he's just on board to do the writing."

"And you're sure you've never met this girl? Not a woman scorned or anything?" Elsa asked. She knew Elgin well enough to know this wasn't likely. Elgin had exotic sexual appetites, but was very discrete about how he satisfied them. Money bought silence just as effectively as it loosened tongues, and money accompanied by the threat of violence bought even more silence. Kiss and tell didn't seem nearly so attractive when it was accompanied by the possibility of never being able to look in a mirror again for fear of what you might see looking back at you.

"No. If that had been the case I would have recognised her at the time of the interview."

"OK then." Langsdorf steepled his fingers and rested his chin on them. "We have three people, two identified, and whose locations we know, or at least where we can locate them if we want to. The third, though, makes violence a risky business. If anything happens to the two men we still have the woman to deal with. We don't know her motivation any more than we know Rycroft's. We don't know how much she knows, or how much she can prove. The only safe course of action is to believe she can hurt us badly if she chooses to."

"You don't think that we should silence Nevis and Rycroft then?" asked Elgin.

"Oh yes, I do think we should, but not until we can locate the girl and make sure we get her as well. Has she been seen recently?"

"No." Elgin replied.

"The only sighting we've had appears to be at the constituency office. She could even have been a temp hired for the day." Peters suggested "We never even realised that she might be part of this until a few minutes ago." She looked sideways at Elgin. Unusual for him to miss a detail like that. Was he starting to lose his grip? she wondered.

"No, I don't think so." Elgin stated, with some certainty. "Nevis seemed to know her reasonably well. I remember she was prompting him to ask certain questions, taking notes as I made particular points. My gut feeling is that she knew what she was doing, and he was the amateur."

"Someone working for Rycroft, perhaps?" Langsdorf let the possibility sit there.

"Someone like him would have a full time PA." Said Peters.

"Yes, good thought. Tim, get your rottweiller, Davis, to check out that angle. Metro TV would be a good place to start."

The meeting drew to a close. Peters and Elgin left Langsdorf enjoying an expensive Cognac in the hotel bar, while they went up to Peters' suite to finish the evening off.

"Otto doesn't seem too concerned about this business." Elgin mused.

Elsa Peters raised her head, interrupting what she was doing. "Otto is used to far worse than this. You know that."

"But this time its me in the firing line, not him in some board room putsch. That makes a big difference."

"Only to you, darling." Elsa returned to her task, which was primarily to calm Elgin down and stop him doing anything stupid that might risk her own future. She stopped again. "Shall I get another girl in? I know a new one, a really pretty Chinese, very inventive. She'll do a double act with me if you want her to." Whether Elsa Peters wanted to was taken for granted, she knew.

Elgin grunted, his mind clearly elsewhere. That worried Elsa Peters. If the thought of a novel sexual experience couldn't distract Elgin then things were very serious indeed.

Peters slid herself up the bed until her head rested on Elgin's shoulder. "What's the matter, honey?" she cooed.

"For the first time in my life I'm really scared. Those photos of Camilla, what we've seen in those drafts of the book, the video tape. This isn't just political ruin, this is prison time. I'm not talking about a few month in Ford Open, either. If they join up all the dots it'll be Maximum Security. Can you imagine what it would be like for me, Deputy Prime Minister, in a prison that's full of the sort of criminals that hate people like me on principal."

"Don't worry so much. You're a good looking man, I'm sure you'll find some big butch con to look after you."

"Don't be disgusting, and don't be flippant. This is worse than you can ever imagine."

Elsa lifted Elgin's hand off his chest and slid it down her body to his groin. "Now, now. Poor baby. Let me make it better." The thought of prison worried Elsa Peters as well, but she knew her best chance of safety was by keeping Elgin calm and focused.

"It'll take more than a quick fuck to make this better." Elgin withdrew her hand and climbed out of the bed. He stamped out of the room. Elsa heard the tinkle of glass as the door of the mini-bar was wrenched open.

"Bring me a glass of wine." Elsa called. There was no response.

After a minute or so it was clear that Elgin wasn't returning to the bedroom. Elsa wrapped herself in the crumpled top sheet and walked through to the sitting room of the suite.

Elgin was hunched over, his head in his hands. His body was heaving with sobs of self pity.

Oh dear, thought Elsa. This is going to take considerably more than a lesbian show with a Chinese hooker. She walked across and crouched down beside Elgin's chair. She pulled his head into her shoulder, making the sort of cooing noises mothers make to their children. Elgin wrapped his arms around her and buried his face in the nape of Elsa' neck.

"Come with Mamma." She coaxed him upright, and turned him towards the bedroom. "Mamma's got what you need." As she walked Elgin slowly towards the bedroom door she reached out for her handbag, hoping she had remembered to stock it with Elgin's drugs of choice.

As she searched the handbag with one hand she thumbed through the directory on her mobile 'phone, until she eventually reached the number she looking for. She prayed that the Chinese girl was as good as she had been told.

CHAPTER THIRTEEN

Davis may have been a thug, but he knew how to turn on the charm when he wanted to. Tracy's contacts in the world of motorcycle couriers got him a package destined for delivery to Metro TV's South Bank offices. A wad of £20 notes made sure there would be no questions asked about what he wanted the package, and its documentation, for.

Now he stood in the foyer of the Metro TV building, next to the reception desk, while the package was hand delivered to the relevant department. The excuse that he was to wait to see if there was a reply was sufficient to allow him to loiter in the foyer. It was a common enough instruction. Davis used the time to chatter to the receptionist like a star struck teenager. He made a point of picking out Rycroft's photo from the array of Metro TV's current crop of talent that was displayed around the walls of the reception area.

"My Dad thinks he the greatest since Richard Dimbleby, whoever he was." Gushed Davis.

"He's a nice bloke, too." Offered the receptionist.

"Good looking guy, I'snt he. Bet all the girls fall at his feet, too."

"He doesn't seem to have many female admirers, that I've seen."

"That's unusual, isn't it. Him being on telly and all that."

"He doesn't encourage women. He's very polite though."

"Come on, you can tell me. I bet he's got a girl friend. It's you isn't it?"

The woman simpered. She was 50 at least, but the idea of being Steven Rycroft's girlfriend obviously appealed. "No. Don't be silly. The only girl I've ever seen him with is his PA. Valerie. She's a nice girl. Very pretty."

"Valerie, that's a nice name. I know a girl called Valerie that works here. It isn't the same one is it?"

The receptionist gave Davis the sort of look that suggested it was unlikely that any friend of Davis, male or female, might appeal to Steven Rycroft. "Valerie Mayfield is her full name. What's your friends name?"

"No, she's Valerie Thompson. Come to think of it, it isn't here that she works, its at GMTV." Davis had spotted the messenger leaving the lift, and knew he wouldn't have time to dig any deeper. At least he had a name, and that was a start.

The messenger informed Davis that there was no return package, which suited Davis. Getting it back into the courier company's system would have been an unnecessary waste of his time. He took his leave of the receptionist, and left the building.

*   *   *

The next part of the plan didn't take quite as much organising. Tracy bought a huge bunch of flowers and faked a card to suggest they were from a gentleman admirer. She arrived at Metro TV's reception the next morning and made it clear she was to deliver the flowers to Valerie Mayfield in person, and no one else.

Davis had guessed that Valerie wouldn't be in the building. The fact that the woman hadn't appeared on their radar before meant that she hadn't been seen arriving or leaving with Rycroft, which would have been a natural occurrence at some point if they were working together in the same building. Rycroft had a lot of meetings around London and it would be natural for his PA to accompany him from time to time. She had to be hiding somewhere else. That meant that, if Tracy's performance was convincing enough, Steven Rycroft himself would probably appear to take possession of the flowers.

As a precaution Tracy had covered her natural blond hair with a dark wig, and added a pair of heavy rimmed glasses. The lenses made her squint a little, but Davis considered that would add to the disguise. The glasses also helped to conceal another of the bruises that Davis had left her with.

A soft "bing" announced the arrival of the elevator at the reception level, and Tracy turned to see who came out.

Bingo, she thought. Steven Rycroft himself was walking directly towards her across the reception area.

"I understand you have some flowers for a colleague of mine?" he inquired.

The huge bunch of flowers that Tracey still cradled in her arms was a bit of a giveaway, she thought, but decided not to be cheeky about it. "Yes Sir. I'm to give them to her and no one else, Sir. The gentleman was most insistent."

"That presents a bit of a problem, I'm afraid. Tracey isn't here at present she's …. off sick" Rycroft improvised.

"If you give me her address I'll deliver them to her home. That's no problem, all part of the service."

"I'm sorry, we can't give out employee's home addresses to strangers I'm afraid. I'm sure you wouldn't like it if your boss gave out your address to anyone that walked into the shop."

Tracey chuckled, as she knew she would be expected to. "Quite right too. We get all sorts of weirdoes coming in. Problem is, what am I going to do with the flowers? The gentleman paid a lot of money for them, and I can't take them back to him."

"Tell you what. I'll take the flowers and put them in a taxi. I'll pay, of course. How does that sound?"

"OK, as long as I see you do it."

Steven Rycroft went across and spoke to the receptionist, asking her to ring for a taxi on his account, whispering the address to her at the same time.

The taxi arrived as quickly as only an important client can expect, and Steven Rycroft accompanied the florist's assistant, as he thought of her, out to hand the precious cargo over.

"You know the address?" Rycroft asked the driver, as the girl put the flowers in the back of the cab.

"Yes, Guv, its …"

"No need to tell me," interjected Rycroft. "So long as you know where you're to go."

"No problem Guv, they're as good as delivered." Palming the £5 note that Rycroft had proffered through the open window, the driver swung his cab across the traffic and headed towards Southwark Bridge.

Had Rycroft not turned back towards the Metro TV building so quickly he might have noticed a motorcycle pull out of a side turning and tuck itself behind the taxi, but he had spent enough time so far sorting out Valerie's flowers and now Rycroft just wanted to get back to work.

Rycroft drew another £5 note from his wallet and passed it to the girl. "All happy now?" he asked.

The girl took the note and tucked it in the pocket of her jeans. "That's great Sir. Thanks for your help. I hope she likes them. I picked them out myself." That the last statement was actually true would have come as a surprise to Rycroft, had he known what he had just been a party to. Instead he returned to his office in ignorance of the danger he had placed not just Valerie in, but himself and Nevis as well.

*　　*　　*

The arrival of flowers so unexpectedly firstly delighted Valerie, than immediately made her suspicious. The card said from a "Secret Admirer", and at first Valerie thought they might be from Nevis. Then she thought again.

Steven had 'phoned her to say the flowers were on their way across by taxi, but Nevis knew she wasn't working from the Metro TV office at the moment. OK, he didn't know her home address, or the address of the flat where she was working, but a quiet chat with Steven would have sorted that out. If he had bought the flowers they would have been delivered direct to the apartment.

Another secret admirer? Possible, she supposed, but unlikely. She hadn't really been anywhere recently where she would come to anyone's attention. She could hardly remember the last time she had been in a pub or a club, and someone spotting her in a supermarket wouldn't have known she worked at Metro TV. OK, there was still an outside chance that it could be someone she had spoken to, or a friend of a friend, but she doubted it.

On impulse she crossed to the window. The apartment she was working in was on the first floor, with a bay window that allowed good views along the road in both directions.

The road was a quiet residential side street near Ladbroke Grove. At this time of day she wouldn't expect to see anyone on it except for housewives and nannies. What she did see was a motorbike, parked at the kerb, 50 yards away along the road from the house. She didn't know the residents well, nor any of their regular visitors, but she was sure she hadn't seen the bike before.

Across the road the house opposite had a neatly cut box hedge projecting above its low front wall. At the end of the short hedge stood a wrought iron gate allowing access to a concrete path and the front door.

The day wasn't particularly sunny, but there was enough sunlight breaking through the cloud to cast shadows and across the concrete path, behind the wrought iron gate, was the shadow of what just might be a crouching man.

There was one way to find out. She returned to the desk and picked up her mobile 'phone. She didn't have to look up the three digit number.

"Yes, Police please." She responded to the voice that answered her call.

Valerie quickly gave her details, putting a lot of panic into her voice that she had to admit she was starting to feel. Valerie had heard a lot of complaints about the police, but she had to admit that they responded quickly enough to her call.

The man must have heard the patrol car's siren as it approached, because he took off at speed, running to his motorbike and trying to kick-start it before the police could reach him.

The biker had taken his crash helmet off while he crouched behind the hedge, and now struggled to get it back on again. Facing directly towards Valerie his face was clear to her, and she would later give quite an accurate description of it to the police.

The man finally got his crash helmet on correctly and jerked the bike in to gear, passing the police car as it turned into the street. If the police associated the fast disappearing bike with the emergency call that had directed them to the street they didn't take any action against it. Instead the driver pulled his car to a stop and the two occupants climbed out and walked to the door of the house that contained the apartment from where the call had been made.

Valerie told her story, a version of events that was close to the truth. A prowler dressed in motorcycle leathers and crash helmet who had been on his hands and knees in the opposite garden, and who had fled at the approach of the police. One constable took notes while the other investigated the hiding place, but came and re-joined his colleague, making no comment. They asked routine questions, trying to elicit a description of the man and his motor cycle, which Valerie answered as thoroughly as possible.

At last the police went and Valerie gathered her possessions about her. It was clear that her workplace had been compromised, and she would have to go elsewhere. Too bad, she thought. She had liked the little apartment and her friend had been more than hospitable on the days she had worked there, but to stay would put her old school friend at as much risk as she now realised she was.

After a 'phone call to Rycroft to tell him what had happened, and to take instructions on what to do next, she left the apartment, heading towards Ladbroke Grove underground station.

The station platform was deserted as she got onto a train, heading away from the city. She didn't want anyone second guessing her and getting on the train at Westbourne Park, the next stop on the line. She got off the Hammersmith and City Line at the Hammersmith terminal, and walked the short distance to the District Line station to join a Piccadilly Line train which would allow her to complete her journey.

Had Valerie taken the Hammersmith and City Line train in the other direction she would indeed have seen the motorcyclist who had been watching her apartment. Scott Davis had anticipated Valerie leaving her hiding place and taking the underground, but Valerie had made the correct guess, and now she vanished off Scott Davis's radar once again.

*   *   *

Davis and Elgin were in the pub in Shepherds Market once again, discussing the day's events. The early evening crowd ebbed and flowed around them, but no one paid them particular attention.

"You're sure it was her who called the police?" quizzed Elgin.

"I can't be absolutely sure, Boss. It could have been anyone along that road, but I'm pretty sure the cops stopped outside the house where the flowers were delivered."

"I'm getting a bit fed up with the incompetence of you and your associates, Davis. This is the third time you've followed one of this crowd, and the third time you've been spotted."

"Its not our fault boss. Its hard to do an effective observation by yourself, and out in the open. The cops would have taken over a front bedroom and been hidden behind the net curtains, and out on the street there'd be at least 6 of them, swapping and changing all the time. Even changing their clothes and wigs sometimes."

Elgin wasn't mollified, though he had to admit to himself that Davis was right. "Well, we've lost the woman again, and they're not going to fall for the same trick twice, are they? Looks like we'll just have to go after Nevis and Rycroft by themselves, and hope we can flush out the woman separately. We've got her name now. Perhaps I can call in another favour and find out where she's gone."

"That wasn't her place, by the way, Boss. When I got back to the office I did some checking. There's two flats in the house, and Council Tax is paid in completely different names. She must just have been staying there."

"Knowing that doesn't really help us much. We need to know where she normally lives, and hope to catch her at home. If you can find out who pays the Council Tax for those flats, why can't you find out what address she pays her council tax on?"

"Its not that easy Boss. I knew what borough the flat was in, and just made a few calls around till I found someone who knew someone who knew someone that worked for that borough council. I'd have to try every council in Greater London before I could be sure of finding her that way. She might not even live in London, she could commute in from just about anywhere in South East England."

"What about Metro TV. Can you get access to their employee records?"

"Risky Boss. It would have to be a break in, or at least a distraction job while I looked through the filing cabinets. Might not even be on paper any more, might be on a computer, which is even harder to get into. Besides, she's Rycroft's PA. He might employ her himself, directly, in which case he will have the records, and we know he's cleared out his house in Fulham after our break in."

"Keep your voice down, you fool." The use of the words "break in" had caused a couple of heads to turn in their direction, if only fleetingly. "Ok, keep a close eye on Nevis, and do your best to try to track down where Rycroft disappears to at night. I'll consult with Otto and Elsa, and see what they suggest now."

With that Davis considered himself dismissed and headed for his home. It had been a long and eventful day, and Davis was in need of some creature comforts. Tracy was out that evening, visiting her Mum, and her dopey brother was with her. Davis knew he wouldn't see them before the last train had departed. Davis thumbed through the directory on his mobile 'phone until a name caught his eye. Smiling, he rang the number and offered an invitation to the person that answered his call. The woman knew better than to refuse.

CHAPTER FOURTEEN

"I don't see what else we can do. They have to go." Otto Langsdorf expressed his opinion. "We have worked too hard, come too far to lose it all now."

"It's not as simple as that." Elsa Peters said, angrily. "They obviously have a lot of information, that all has to disappear as well. If the police find that then we may as well walk into Bellmarsh and slam the door closed behind us."

"You're both right." Timothy Elgin tried to calm things down between the brother and sister. "We can't just arrange for them to have an accident and not expect some sort of investigation. The woman, Valerie Mayfield, will take whatever she has straight to the police. Even if the two men appear to be unconnected she will make sure the police find the connection."

"So how do we arrange it then?" Peters asked.

"I'll leave that to Davis. That's his area expertise, and frankly I don't want to know how he does it. But he also has to find the girl. We have to assume that she has a full set of files. We also have to find where Rycroft has been hiding out, because he will no doubt have kept his files close at hand."

"OK, that's the hard part, but we can deal with Nevis now, can't we?" Langsdorf asked.

"Yes. I think we can. So long as we get his laptop and anything else he has in his hotel room."

"The last time you took his laptop was a disaster." Peters commented.

"Yes, I'm afraid it was, but we don't have to have what's on the hard drive. We only have to be able to destroy it, and any discs or flash drives he might have. We learnt that lesson the hard way, but I'll make sure Davis understands what he's got to do."

"They may go to the police; Rycroft and the girl. You know, when Nevis…. you know." Langsdorf 's voice tailed off into silence, unwilling to utter the word.

"They might, but I don't think they will. They'll think Nevis has just disappeared, run out on them. It's what I would think." Elgin chewed on his thumb nail for a moment, deep in thought. His face brightened. "Yes. That will be when they make the mistakes that will lead us to them. They'll go looking for him, and that's when we'll get them."

"You had better be right about that." Growled Langsdorf. He stood up. "OK, I'll leave you two to your own devices." He leered across the room at Elgin, but his expression wasn't seen. " I've got things I need to be doing." With that he left the hotel room.

Peters waited for the door to shut, then moved from her chair and stretched herself out across the bed, lying on her side to look across at Elgin, who still sat chewing on his thumb nail. "It will be OK. Tim. Once Davis has sorted the three of them out we'll be free and clear."

"Elsa, I really wish I could be that confident. There are so many questions not answered. How did they find out about us anyway? We covered our tracks well enough, didn't we?"

Peters lifted her bottom and wriggled out of her skirt before replying. "When more than one person knows a secret then it isn't a secret any more. Look how many people we've had to pay off. It was inevitable that someone would talk eventually."

"And we left traces." Elgin added. "Every time Otto did a deal there was a trail of connections that led back. Follow the money, isn't that what they say?"

Peters had unbuttoned her blouse and allowed it to fall open, her generous silk clad breasts assisting gravity to push the material aside. "But the money only goes back as far as a numbered bank account. Once it gets there those very discrete Cayman Islanders make sure that the trail goes cold." Peters lay back on the bed, her head sinking into the pillows. "Now, come over here and let me calm you down."

Elgin ignored her. "The money trail stops, but not the connections. I've been thinking. Pretty much every deal we've done my name has been linked with it in some way. Oh, maybe not directly, but I've always known one of the players. Take that Asian business. Not only did I sign the contract, but I've been seen with the Chief Executive; Had my photo taken with him."

"Relax honey. Please. You're a big league politician, you're seen with loads of business people, and civil servants, and other politicians, and have your photo taken a dozen times a day. If every person you met was bent then the prisons would be full to overflowing with people who have shaken your hand. We've been very selective about who we've dealt with. They have as much to lose as you do. I can't see any of them rushing to the police any time soon. And ultimately the trail stops with me, not you. You can always claim you knew nothing about what was going on. Now," she patted the bed next to her and opened her legs invitingly. "Come to Momma."

*   *   *

Scott Davis walked into then pub and placed his usual order: A pint of lager and a double scotch with ice. He smiled at the pretty New Zeelander who served him and she gave him a professional smile back, before turning her back to put the payment into the cash register. She handed Davis his change, hardly even looking at him, and drifted back to the corner of the bar where her e-book sat waiting for her. Davis was the only customer in the pub.

Davis went over and settled into the booth at the back of the pub, where he could see who came and went. Langsdorf entered a few minutes later and walked straight across to sit opposite his employee.

Elgin took a big gulp of his drink before speaking. That was a danger signal as far as Davis was concerned. There was going to be some messy work to do, he felt sure.

"Nevis has to go, as soon as you can arrange it."

"Can I be sure exactly what you mean by that?" Davis asked. "It's my neck on the line if I don't get your meaning properly."

"Go. Vanish. Be no more. Does that make it clearer? Never to be seen again. By anyone, anywhere."

"You want me to kill him?"

Elgin went white and frantically looked around to see if Davis had been overheard. "You fool, keep your voice down."

"Relax, the place is empty and she" Davis jerked his thumb towards the barmaid, "is far more interested in her book than she is in us."

"Never the less, keep your voice down. Just being seen with you right now is risky enough. " Elgin cleared his throat, readying himself to face up to his true intentions. "Yes, that is what I mean. But you have to make sure you clean up afterwards. You have to get everything he's been working on. That means papers, computers, discs, anything he may have touched. If there's one thing left that links him to me its curtains, and I'll make sure you go down with me. Clear?"

"Clear Boss. I understand, don't worry. Pity they've already had them Olympics."

"What's that got to do with anything?"

"Construction sites always provide useful places to dispose of bodies. They say that half the supports on the Hammersmith flyover are filled with people who upset the Krays."

"Well, you'll have to find somewhere else. Just make sure that if he's ever found it will look like an accident or suicide."

Elgin swallowed the remainder of his scotch and slammed the glass down, the sudden noise making the barmaid jump and look across at him. He left the booth without saying goodbye and headed through the doorway and walked towards Piccadilly.

* * *

I try to get as much exercise each day as I can, and therefore take the stairs from the hotel lobby to my room. It's only a few flights, but taken at speed it raises my heart rate a little, which is what I want it to do. Most of the other guests, on the other hand, tend to use the speedy elevator service to get to the level on which their rooms are located. I was therefore quite surprised to find two men coming through the doors to the third floor stairwell as I reached them.

I stood to one side to let them pass but they stopped dead, in front of the doors, blocking my way. This didn't feel good. They didn't look good.

I shouldn't be judgemental, I know, and I shouldn't think in stereotypes. All sorts of people stay in hotels, and good looks and nice clothes aren't a pre-requisite for the booking of a hotel room. But these two looked as out of place as baked beans on toast at a Royal banquet. Both men were big, well over 6 ft tall. They were also stocky. Had they been standing outside a night club, wearing dark glasses in the middle of the night, they would have fitted in.

At the moment they wore jeans above heavy work boots. I had a feeling the boots had steel toe caps, and they weren't to prevent their tootsies being crushed if something fell on them. You took care around people like this to make sure you never dropped anything near their feet. It could be the last thing you ever drop.

Above the jeans they wore identical black zip up jackets made of some shiny sort of material. Above the collars hung the hood of whatever was being worn beneath the jacket. There were no dark glasses. These men wanted me to see their eyes, and they wanted me to see the violence that lurked behind them. Finally the men's heads were clean shaven, which added more menace. If you ordered a stock caricature violent thug from central casting then this is what you would get. No, correction, with a stock character you wouldn't get so many tattoos and scars – no one would believe any person could have so many. If tattoos and scars were rationed, then these two had cornered the market.

"Er, excuse me." I ventured, hopefully. I stepped to one side, trying to reach the door handle behind them. They made no reply, but did take half a step towards me.

"Er, look, I don't want any trouble." I tried again. "If you want my wallet you can have it. I won't call the police, I promise."

"We don't want your money, Mr Nevis." I thought I felt the floor vibrate as he growled at me. They knew my name, so this was no random mugging. "You can come with us quietly, or you can come with us unconscious. It's your choice."

"Why should I come with you at all?" I stammered. I felt a warm trickle run down my leg. I hoped it was sweat, but I couldn't be sure.

"Because someone wants you to come with us, and we've been paid very well to make sure you do. Now be a good boy, turn round and go down the stairs to the very bottom. Don't try to run, because you won't get very far." To demonstrate why I wouldn't get far he pulled the bottom of his jacket up to reveal the butt of a gun protruding from the waist band of his jeans.

His partner spoke for the first time. "We've been told not to shoot you….. unless it's absolutely necessary."

My shoulders sagged as I realised that I had no choice. I turned and started to walk slowly back down the stairs, pausing at each corner so that they two thugs could keep pace. I didn't want them to panic and do something they would regret, and which I would regret even more.

As I ventured below the lobby level of the hotel stairs the carpet on the floor ended abruptly, and the pleasant cream paint with the horizontal gold stripe gave way to institutional green. The polished wooden hand rail became plain metal with chipped black paint. At the bottom I was faced with a set of double doors which were scarred by years of hotel staff banging solid objects into them as they pushed them open.

"Keep going." Rumbled a voice behind me. I knew it was now or never.

I pushed one of the doors open and stepped through, holding the door to prevent it swinging shut. One of the thugs, the one with the gun, stepped ahead of his partner to follow me through. I swing the door with all my might and felt it crack against his head. He let out a curse, which rang in my ears as I legged it down the corridor. It was only at this point that I realised that I had no idea in which direction safety lay.

A bang echoed along the corridor and I realised that the threat to shoot me hadn't been idle. Something smacked into the floor ahead of me and pinged away into the gloom. I realised with some relief that the corridor was very poorly lit, which wouldn't help anyone's aim.

The slap and echo of my running feet meant that I couldn't hear if they were chasing. A corner loomed out of the shadows and I thumped into a wall as I tried to change direction without slowing. Ouch. That would hurt in the morning, if I lived to see the morning. A second bullet slammed into the wall where my head had been a fraction of a second before, as my feet gathered traction to propel me forward once again.

A door appeared ahead of me, light beaming across the corridor to illuminate the wall opposite it. I slid to a stop and yanked frantically at the handle, my panic rising as it refused to budge. Then data filtered into my fear stricken brain and I made sense of the word printed in black on gold above the handle. I reacted to it and stopped pulling and pushed instead. I half stepped and half fell into the steamy noise of the hotel's kitchen.

"Oi, who you." A voice challenged me. "You no allowed here." Then the man stepped towards me to block my path. Something behind me caught his eye and I saw fear cloud over them. I turned to see thug number one standing in the doorway, the hand hanging down by his side still holding the gun. He realised what the kitchen labourer was looking at and hurriedly put his hand behind his back. A second member of the kitchen staff came over to join us, curious about what was going on.

The thug put up his left hand, clearly signalling to thug number two to stop before he got to the door. A third person, this one dressed in chef's whites and hat, started towards us. Thug number one stepped away from the door and headed back the way he had come.

"What's going on here?" The chef asked, his strong Lancashire accent somehow reassuring. "Who was he?"

"Sorry, he tried to rob me. I just ran."

"One of them had gun, Chef." The first kitchen hand offered.

"OK. I'll call the police." The Chef turned to go towards an office. There was no messing around with this guy. He was in charge of his kitchen, and that was that. I realised that the thick walls of the kitchen and the noise of food preparations and cooking meant that they probably hadn't heard the two shots. They also hadn't seen the second man. Time for damage limitation.

"No, please. No need for that. He didn't get anything, and he'll be long gone by now, I'm sure. Not much point involving the police."

"OK, if that's what you want. But I'll have to call the duty manager. Armed men running around below stairs, we can't have that, can we? And we certainly can't have it in my kitchen. I've got a dining room full of hungry people, and haven't got time for that sort of nonsense."

"OK. Look I'm in room 320. If the manager wants to speak to me that's where I'll be." Just for as long as it takes me to pack my bags, I didn't add.

"OK. Well, you better not go back that way" he nodded towards the corridor, " just in case. Yusuf, show him where the service elevator is. Make sure he gets back to his room safely" With that the Chef turned on his heel and headed towards the office. Yusuf beckoned to me to follow. I tried not to notice the large knife that he picked up as he passed a preparation table.

*   *   *

I placated the Duty Manager and assured her I would take no action against the hotel for the breach of security. That seemed to satisfy her and she went off to deal with more urgent matters, such as preparing my bill. She clearly wasn't unhappy that I had chosen to leave. Whether she guessed that I had been specifically targeted or not I didn't know, but she clearly saw me a s a problem, and one she was quite content to allow to walk out through the hotel door. She promised a discount as compensation for the hotel's security failure, and left my room.

I rang Steven Rycroft and told him of the development.

"You think its related to us, to the book?"

"What do bears do in the woods? I don't think there can be any doubt. They're rattled, no doubt about it. They probably think we sent those photos to the press, and that's what's triggered this attempt. We've got them on the run, and they're getting desparate."

"What do you think they were going to do? Maybe they just wanted to warn you off?"

"No, I think it was more serious. If they wanted to warn me off they could have done it much more easily. A horse's headed my bed would have been loud and clear."

Steven snorted. "Yes, an attempted kidnapping was a bit over the top. So what do you think would have happened?"

"I'm pretty sure I wouldn't have been seen again."

"Yes, it's possible suppose. Did they get into your room?"

"No. I think they would have done what they needed to, then taken my keys and come back for my laptop and so on. They would have got the memory stick as well."

"I suggest you make a copy and put it into a safe deposit box. You can post the key to me at Metro and I'll make sure it's safe."

"How do you know they won't come after you next?"

"I'm sure I would have been next, and probably Valerie after me. No, I'll make sure that if anything happens to me the deposit box key gets to someone who knows what to do with the information."

I agreed the course of action, and made my preparations to leave. I had already discussed my method of exit with the Duty Manager and felt reasonably sure that I wouldn't be followed again.

*   *   *

Davis rang Timothy Elgin to let him know about the aborted murder attempt.

Elgin sighed deeply. "OK, call your dogs off. He's going to be very careful from now on, and we daren't risk another attempt. He may go to the police, and we can't show ourselves. Can your boys be traced back to you?"

"No. It was arranged over the phone with a trusted third party. They didn't know who they were working for, and even if they did they aren't the sort to talk. Do you think Nevis will go to the police?"

"I hope not. I don't think they're ready to go public yet, and a police investigation will get in their way. I'll make some discrete inquiries, but I don't think we'll hear any more about it."

"OK, boss, anything else?"

"Yes. This is another failure Davis. You're starting to look accident prone. You understand me?"

"Yes, Boss. Look, it was a bit of bad luck, that's all. The boys were a bit too trusting, they didn't think Nevis would make a run for it."

"We can't afford bad luck Davis. Make sure you have better luck in the future." The line went dead as Elgin terminated the conversation.

Scott Davis returned to the party he had been attending, surrounded by people who would provide him with an alibi if he needed one. A girl draped herself around him, but he pushed her away angrily. Elgin had made a clear threat, and Davis didn't like that. Maybe it was time that Mr Elgin realised who held the power in their relationship.

Davis grinned an evil grin and pulled the girl that he had previously rebuffed towards him and put his arm around her, squeezing her buttock. "let's find somewhere a bit quieter" he breathed into her ear. He took her hand and pulled her towards the door.

CHAPTER FIFTEEN

My meeting with the man from the Ministry was straight out of a cheap spy novel. I was told to go to Primrose Hill and sit on a particular park bench. I would be contacted. My contact, Miles Frobisher, was straight out of the same spy novel. He was tall, mid fifties, slim and elegantly dressed in a navy pinstripe suit, briefcase in one hand and rolled umbrella in the other. The only thing missing was the bowler hat set at a jaunty angle, but fashions do change, I suppose, even in spy novels. He took a seat beside me.

Holding his finger to his lips to silence me, he reached into his brief case and took out a cheap transistor radio, which he switched on. Rock music blared out, scaring the scavenging pigeons. He slipped the radio inside my open coat.

"Just a precaution, you understand. He explained "Mr, er ....".

"Wesley." I interjected.

"Er, yes, quite so, Mr *Wesley*. This meeting isn't taking place, and if forced to do so I shall say that on oath."

"There could be a camera hidden in the bushes." I countered, trying to prevent him thinking he was in absolute control."

"And that will show what, precisely?" He reached into his briefcase again, and took out a plastic lunch box. "Even senior civil servants are entitled to eat lunch in the park. Now, to business. And even senior civil servants might strike up a conversation with someone that they're sharing a park bench with." He opened the lunch box and delicately extracted a sandwich. It was one of those tiny triangular ones that the average person wolfs down in two mouthfuls, but he made it last until the meeting was finished.

"You may be wondering why I changed my mind about meeting you. In truth I had no intention of ever seeing you, but things happen that can change one's mind. In this case I was curious. Something that I was sure I had closed forever had managed to open itself again. I wondered why, and so I sent for the file. It couldn't be found. That worried me."

"Files do go astray." I commented.

"The cover of this file was a deep red colour. That may mean nothing to a lay person, but in my world such files are only passed from hand to hand, and every time that happens signatures are exchanged. For such a file to *go astray* is unthinkable. No, it has been removed, and whoever removed it, I feel sure, is not acting in the national interest. If they were they would have asked me to remove the file. I have launched an investigation of course, but I don't expect it to reveal anything." He took a tiny nibble of his sandwich.

"I then asked the Ministry of Defence Police for their copy of the file on the subject. How they became involved will be revealed later. Their copy too had gone missing. Someone wants to make sure that this matter remains a secret, so much so that they don't even trust loyal servants such as me to protect the file. That can only mean, as far as I am concerned, that someone very, very important nearly got their fingers burnt. If that is the case, they must have been playing with fire. As such I feel no great need to protect them." He took another minute bite at the sandwich.

"I'm going to tell you a story. You may judge for yourself whether it is true or not, I will not comment either way. First, however, you must understand a little of how Defence Procurement works. It is a very small world, with very few companies trusted to undertake contracts. If, for example, we need a new aeroplane building we go to British Aerospace and ask them to build it. BAe, however, won't do all the work themselves. The electrics will be sub contracted to someone like Lucas, the hydraulics to Dowty, the electronics to someone else, and so on. These are all trusted companies who have undertaken work for the Government for years. However, sub-contractors are required to go through the same exacting vetting process as the principle contractors. If the Ministry isn't happy with them, then we forbid their employment on the contract. Now, we come to SHADOW. Have you heard of it?" I told him that I hadn't.

"No, perhaps it isn't really big enough to attract widespread attention. SHADOW is a new battlefield communications system for the army. As usual, the tendering process attracted the companies that we expected it to, and the principle contract was awarded without any difficulty. Then one of the sub-contractors withdrew, for no apparent reason. A new company entered the arena, bidding for the work. We shall call them ABC Systems, for the sake of a name. The Ministry knew nothing much about them, so we appointed a Procurement Manager, we'll call him John, to investigate them. John went to see the company, interviewed the senior managers, reviewed their security, their accounts and so on. All very routine so far. The company took John out to dinner, again routine. So long as the meal isn't too lavish, and so long as John recorded the fact that he had received hospitality, then there was no cause for concern.

As it happens, the meal was satisfactory, and not too expensive. At the end of it most of the company executives departed, leaving just two people with John. They encouraged him to stay, and plied him with wine. We'll call these two people Jack and Jill. They started talking about how difficult life was for public servants, how poor the salaries are in comparison to private enterprise, how ungrateful the politicians are, and so on. They persuaded John to go to a night club with them. Well, I say *night club*, it was actually a lap dancing club. They were joined by a couple of young ladies, whose role in life could only be imagined at in such a place. The talk went on. Its all terribly unoriginal, I'm afraid. The Russians were doing all that in the 1960's to try to recruit junior clerks into spying for them. However, it still works with the right target. Fortunately, John wasn't the right target.

John realised that an attempt was being made to compromise him, and eventually managed to make his excuses and leave. The following day he submitted a full written report to his line manager, who immediately contacted me. I contacted the Ministry of Defence Police, and we established a plan to mount a *sting* operation. John was asked to take leave, and we put the story around that he was suffering from stress. We replaced him with an undercover police officer, complete with back up surveillance team, and notified ABC Systems that their case was being handled by the new man, we'll call him Jim.

I was surprised when I received a call from the Minister for Defence Procurement, asking what was going on. This was a small part of a medium sized project, something that Ministers have no need to get involved in. The principle contract had been signed already, and this sort of minor change of a sub-contractor is hardly unusual. The calls came every day. What was happening? Why the delay? I got the impression the Minister was under some pressure from somewhere, but I couldn't imagine why. With the benefit of hind sight it explains matters a little, perhaps, but at that time I thought he was just being over zealous.

Jim made contact with the company, and in due course he went to meet with the company management again. The dinner routine was repeated, as was the trip to the lap dancing club. Jim was wired, I think the expression is, of course, and there was a hidden camera never far away from him. He pretended to play along, being careful not to say anything that might be interpreted as entrapment. A second meeting was arranged. Only Jack turned up to it, and he handed over an envelope containing £10,000. Our surveillance people spotted their surveillance man, or should I say woman. We had anticipated them trying to get photographs, for possible blackmail at a later date. Its what we would have done if we had been them.

We put all the evidence before the Minister the next day. He was clearly rattled, but again I failed to register it at as anything significant. He should have been delighted that we had uncovered a major attempt at corruption, but the Minister treated us as though we had handed him a live rattle snake. A couple of days later I was summoned by the Minster, and told to bury the whole thing, and bury it deep. I should warn off the offending company, of course, but the Government didn't want any scandal emerging. It was a delicate time, the Minister said, and the Government could do without any embarrassment. Its always a delicate time for Governments, of course, but the story held up, at that time.

I presented the evidence to the company the next day. They were deeply embarrassed, of course, and swore that Jack and Jill didn't actually work for them, they had no idea what they had been doing, etc. They said they were just a couple of PR consultants who had over stepped the mark. We advised them never to bid for Government work again and left it at that. The files were closed and locked away in a deep archive. The matter was finished with, or so I thought, until your telephone call." Frobisher popped the last morsel of his sandwich into his mouth and brushed non-existent crumbs off his lap.

I realised that Frobisher was making preparations to leave. "What about Jack and Jill? Do they have real names?" I wanted to glean the maximum amount of information from him. He paused, deliberating on whether he should tell me.

"Are you keen ion cross words?" I said I was. "Good. Think of a lioness, in a film about lions, and add the name of a Great Russian Tsar. That's the woman. The man, now let me see. Ah yes. A 19th century Scottish author and poet, and a famous Welsh rugby fly half."

"Is there somewhere I could start looking to find more *stories* like this?" So far I still had nothing linking this case to Elgin. I was getting desperate. I didn't think he would answer, so I was surprised when he did.

"Try Tan-Kum-Doc." he said enigmatically. He reached for the transistor radio. "Goodbye, Mr … er, Wesley. We shan't meet again." He turned on his heel and marched away down the hill.

I'm actually not a great one for crosswords. The Daily Mail is about the limits of my capabilities, but the clues he had given me weren't difficult. I put Elsa together with Peter, and Scott with Davis. My link with Elgin still wasn't established. However, I did have another chapter of the book, even if Frobisher denied everything. Well, I am writing a work of fiction, aren't I?

*   *   *

Newspapers maintain informal links with their counterparts abroad. It helps when covering stories in foreign countries, without all the expense of having to pay for resident reporters. E-mails were exchanged, along with a promise of generous rewards if Camilla Elgin could be tracked down. Tunisia isn't a wealthy country, despite its thriving tourist industry, and rumour of a reward travels fast in such a place.

A waiter approached a local reporter and asked to look at the photograph that was being shown around the coffee houses. He told the reporter that he was sure that the woman was staying at the hotel where he worked. The reporter visited the hotel himself to make a positive identification. A 'phone call to the British reporter and his photographer companion brought them hurrying from the city in a taxi. A woman was pointed out, reclining on a sun lounger. Cash was handed over.

A shadow passed across the woman's face, and she opened her eyes. It didn't take the inappropriate northern European clothing to tell her who she was looking at. She was a politician's wife, and could spot a reporter at a hundred yards.

"Hello boys," She breathed. "What took you so long?"

Camilla stuck to the story that she had agreed with the Number 10 Press Office. She may hate Elgin, now, but she still had to be careful. If she made him angry he might cut off her access to her daughters or, even worse, cut off her allowance. Try as he might, the reporter couldn't shift her from the established story. It was all her fault. Timothy Elgin was a saint, and she was a sinner. The photographer snapped a few photo's but Camilla resolutely refused to remove her bikini top. The reporter considered the whole trip a washout, and prepared to leave.

"Do you read books?" Camilla asked the reporter. The incongruity of the question paled into insignificance beside the archness in her voice. The reporter turned back to her and sat down again, giving her his full attention once again.

"Someone's writing a book." explained Camilla. "At the time I left Timothy still wasn't sure who's writing it, but he's a very, very worried man. It's written as fiction, but whoever is writing it has access to some very good sources, and if people start putting two and two together they might just come up with the right answers. How good is your maths?"

"Are you saying that this novel is really all about your husband?" Asked the reporter.

"I'm saying no such thing, but if someone else were to say something like that, it wouldn't be my fault."

"How do we find out who the author is?"

"Ah, that's *your* problem, but I know Timothy was getting close to finding out, he may even have a name by now. I do know that his starting point was a journalist, a Samantha Walker."

"Sexy Sam." Sniggered the photographer.

"You know her?" asked the reporter.

"Half of Fleet Street is trying to get into her knickers." He responded. "Including me, so yes, I know her." The reporter stood up, ready to leave once again.

"Good. Well, thank you Mrs Elgin. We'll leave you to enjoy your holiday, for a little longer at least. I'm sure some of our slower colleagues will be paying you a visit once we've published our photos of you, and the interview. And thanks for the tip off. We'll follow it up."

The two men left, and Camilla called a waiter over. He took her order, making sure he was standing well out of arm's reach. Camilla ordered champagne. Time to move on, she thought. Cyprus sounded like it might be nice.

*   *   *

An internet search revealed that Tan-Kum-Doc was a lake in South East Asia. It was being dammed in order to turn it into a source of hydro electricity, and a further search revealed that National Hydro had won the contract for the work. Clearly Miles Frobisher had heard something to suggest to him that the deal might not be entirely above board.

The following day I went to the public records office in Kew, to see what I could discover about the contract. What I found surprised even me.

CHAPTER SIXTEEN

"She's a woman." I explained to Steven, over the 'phone. Face to face meetings were totally out of the question now.

"Who? Stop talking in riddles man."

"The person responsible for setting up the contract with National Hydro. Its a woman. I doubt she would have been influenced by an evening in a lap dancing club."

"Doesn't mean she didn't take a bribe to sort the contract, though." Steven countered.

"Doesn't mean she did either." I replied. "It doesn't fit the mould described by Frobisher though. He pointed me towards her quite deliberately, so he clearly suspects something."

"We'll have to bluff it out then. Or rather you will. Confront her and see how she reacts."

"I might as well play Russian Roulette. If it goes wrong she could have me in court for defamation of character."

"Unlikely. If she's guilty she won't want the attention. Remember Jonathan Aitkin; Sued for libel: Lost the case and ended up doing time for conspiracy. If she isn't guilty, then she might be able to point you in the direction of the person who is. That must be worth a punt, don't you think."

I agreed with Steven, if somewhat reluctantly. The next problem was how to get access to her. Posing as a journalist was no good this time. She would be likely to run a mile if she was guilty, and if she was innocent she would just direct me to the department's

Press Office. Steven at last hit on an idea. They're so creative, these media types. He ran it by me, and I added a couple of touches of my own.

I rang Valerie and asked her to do a few things for me. I suggested that she come along for the ride. I had no idea what this woman would be like, and if she was on the defensive she might just cry foul, and I wanted a witness.

*   *   *

Valerie and I waited in the restaurant. It was an expensive restaurant. Well, we justified, the senior executive of a multi-national corporation wouldn't eat in Burger King, would he? Gloria Delgado, the civil servant responsible for the awarding of the contract to build a dam in South East Asia, was expecting to meet Ron Hutchinson from National Hydro, to discuss a few points relating to the contract and the flow of funds from the agencies financing the project to his own company. It was a small subterfuge, well, no, a big one I suppose, but a necessary one if we were to get Gloria Delgado to meet with us.

We had no idea what Gloria looked like, so we had left a message at the front desk so that she could be directed to us.

Gloria was a good looking woman in her late thirties. She has a fine figure, as far as can be discerned beneath her conservative working clothes. Her hair was styled and well groomed. She is, as far as I can make out, the perfect female equivalent to Miles Frobisher. I concluded that there must be a mould somewhere that churns out civil servants. The waiter departed, leaving a thoroughly confused Ms Delgado.

"Who are you? I was expecting Mr Hutchinson."

"I'm sorry." I replied, rising to my feet and offering my hand. "My name is John Wesley, and this is my assistant, Valerie. We work for a newspaper, and we're following up on a story relating to National Hydro, a company we believe you're familiar with." We thought it best to keep our cover story reasonably close to the truth.

"You have a damned cheek." Ms Delgado retorted. "I will be reporting this incident to the Press Complaints Commission. Goodbye."

"Very well, Ms Delgado." I called towards her retreating back. "But that just means we'll publish what we have." I bluffed. She stopped, undecided what to do. "I'm sure it would be better if you were to put your side of the story."

She turned and came back to the table. "What are you going to publish?"

"We have strong reason to believe that the National Hydro contract involved corruption at a high level in the agency that you work for, Ms Delgado. We can publish that, and providing we don't name names we can't be sued for libel" I hoped. "Conversely, you can tell us what really happened, and we can publish that." As bluffs go they don't get much bigger, but once you've stared death in the face you tend to take more risks.

Gloria Delgado sat down at the table. She was worried, I could see that.

"We're already quite convinced that you're an innocent victim." Valerie reached forward and laid her hand on Gloria's arm. "But if you don't tell us your side of the story everyone will believe that you're guilty."

Gloria Delgado spent some time thinking about this, chewing her bottom lip in anxiety. For some perverse reason I found this attractive. Funny, I don't remember ever pulling the wings off butterflies when I was a kid.

"Can I have a drink?" Whispered Gloria. "I'm going to need one."

I suppressed a sigh of relief: she was staying. "Of course. What would you like?"

Drinks were ordered, but Gloria declined our offer of food, not surprisingly perhaps. As we waited for service Gloria started to tell her story.

"It all happened by accident, really." She began. "The Tan-Kum-Doc project is internationally funded, as these sort of programmes often are. Britain is putting up about a quarter of the money, as part of our overseas development programme, some is coming from the EU, some from the World Bank, and there is some private finance coming in as well, looking to return a profit from the operation of the dam when it starts to produce electricity. Someone has to act as co-ordinator, so we got the job, primarily because the British Government is the largest single contributor.

This is a high profile programme for the Government, in terms of Britain's commitment to overseas development, so the Government wanted someone high profile involved, on the political side. Because of the amount of time commitment that would be involved the Foreign Secretary couldn't take it on, and the junior Foreign Office Ministers are all too light weight, even the Minister for Overseas Development. So Timothy Elgin was appointed." My ears pricked up. This was one of the few times that we had heard Elgin's name spoken out loud in connection with just about anything. We had thought that he was Teflon Man, totally non-stick.

"I had to travel abroad for several meetings, and Timothy came along to represent the Government. In most cases he was just along for visibility, but when it came time to sign contracts with other major partners, he was the person to do it. Naturally, we spent quite a lot of time together. Its unavoidable on aeroplanes and in hotels. He's an attractive man, I know that isn't an excuse. I betrayed my husband, I know that, but what can I say? I'm a weaker woman than I thought."

So that was it, was it? Not corruption this time, but good old fashioned amour.

"Are you saying that you had an affair with Timothy Elgin?" asked Valerie, wishing to dot the I's and cross the t's.

"Yes. That is what I'm saying, and it led directly to the award of the contract to National Hydro. I did it to help Timothy, that's the only excuse that I can offer. At least I thought that was why I was doing it. I've had some doubts about that since, though." Gloria's glass was empty, so I signalled the waiter for a refill. Gloria offered me a grateful look.

"It was getting time for a decision on the contract to be made. There were several bidders in, including several from European companies. Most of the bids were better than National's. I was at the stage of checking out the credentials of the European bidders, through their parent Governments, when Timothy approached me. Our affair had been running for a few months by this time. We'd see each other once or twice week, usually during the day. One day, after we had … you know," she said coyly, "he told me he was worried about something, and that possibly I could help. I asked him what, telling him I'd gladly do anything he asked. He told me that he was under enormous pressure to make sure that a British company got the Tan-Kum-Doc contract, and the preferred bidder was National Hydro. He asked me if they stood any sort of chance. I said that they didn't, not really. He said that could be very bad for him, bad for his career. I asked how, but he wouldn't say. I think I got the impression he might be being blackmailed. If so then I considered it possible that I might be the grounds for the blackmail."

Very clever, I thought. Make Gloria feel guilty, and she would be putty in Elgin's hands.

"Well, I loved Timothy, or at least I thought I did. So I did what any woman in love would do in my place. No company is totally squeaky clean, and if you look hard enough you can find some reason not to award them a contract. That's what I did. The only companies that emerged as being fit to award the contract too were National Hydro and two companies that were more expensive than them. So the contract went to National Hydro. The irony is that I would have been able to disqualify National quite easily. I had plenty of evidence that they had been involved in bribery abroad before, especially in the Middle East. But of course that all added to the probability that where bribery had failed, they were now indulging in blackmail.

What made me a bit more suspicious was something that happened a couple of weeks after the contract had been signed. I was contacted by a man calling himself Scott Davis. He asked to meet me, and suggested I speak to Timothy if I needed to know why. Timothy urged me to meet Davis, and so I did. He tried to give me an envelope, stuffed full of money. I have no idea how much it was, but it was about an inch thick, and it was all £50 notes. He said I had earned it, and I should take it. He got quite angry when I refused. I wouldn't even touch the envelope, even when he tried to force it into my hand. Timothy was quite angry as well, when I told him, but not for the right reasons. He should have been insulted on my behalf, but he said I should have taken the money. It would have been better all round, he said. I couldn't understand why though. We had a row about it, and we never really recovered from that. The affair was over. We saw each other, oh, perhaps twice more. The last time was really to make sure that I wasn't going to be a nuisance to him, I think."

I thought that Gloria was going to break down in tears, but she is a senior civil servant, and they don't do things like that. She kept herself under tight control. "That's it really. All there is to tell, until I got this call. I was surprised, I can tell you, but the woman I talked to ... Was that you?" she looked at Valerie, who nodded. "Yes, you were most persuasive. Normally those sorts of queries would be handled at a junior level. However, I have to say I was curious."

"You said you had started to get a little, how should I put this? *Suspicious* of Timothy Elgin's involvement? Why was that?"

"I would say doubts, rather than suspicions. Firstly, I found out that Timothy had lobbied very hard to be appointed as Britain's representative. The PM took quite a lot of persuading that Timothy was the most appropriate person. It really should have been either the Foreign Secretary or the Minister for Overseas Development. Secondly it was the whole idea of Timothy being blackmailed. He never said he had been of course, but no would really be in a position to threaten Timothy. Politically he is too powerful, almost untouchable, so blackmail was the only explanation that fitted. But it still didn't ring true. They didn't have to blackmail Timothy, it would have been easier to blackmail me. If I loved him I wouldn't want to see him harmed, and of course I had my own marriage to protect. There's far less risk involved in blackmailing a civil servant than there is in blackmailing a Government minister. If it all blew up it would look like my fault, but if it blew up this way round it would look like Timothy's fault. It isn't conclusive, of course, but that's what I've come to believe."

I made sympathetic noises. "So what happens now?" asked Gloria. "You expose me as a corrupt official, I suppose. Well, I'll get in ahead of you. I'll resign from my post today, as soon as I get back to the office."

"Don't be too hasty." Valerie stepped in quickly. "Look, we believe you're an innocent, well almost innocent, victim in this. We have evidence that Timothy Elgin is at the centre of a web of corruption going back nearly 20 years. If you were to make a clean breast of things, give evidence against him, then you would make a major contribution to justice."

She looked aghast at the suggestion that her beloved Timothy could be such a criminal, but gradually it dawned on her that if her suspicions had been correct, then it was possible that he might be involved in more than just one corrupt deal. "OK, I can see your point, but what should I do?"

"I suggest that you go and see a solicitor, and swear out an affidavit." I proposed. "Keep it to yourself for the time being. When the time is right, you can come forward and offer your evidence to the police. It isn't the right time yet though."

"I agree with, er, John." Valerie struggled to remember my cover name. "You could be in danger if you act in haste. Stay quiet and I'm sure it will all work out in the end." Something else occurred to Valerie. "No doubt you want to save your marriage, and you are probably tempted to confess what you've done to your husband. Again, say nothing for the moment. You can have no idea how your husband might react. If he were to confront Elgin it might give him a warning, and that could be very dangerous for you."

"You've just used the word 'dangerous' twice. What do you mean?"

"We have reason to believe that at least one former associate of Elgin's has died because of what they know about him." I explained. Gloria looked genuinely shocked. "Look, you have nothing to worry about so long as you don't draw attention to yourself. We'll keep this quiet until the time is right. Just keep your nerve, but also keep quiet for the moment." Remembering my own recent experiences I fervently hoped that I was right.

After Gloria left Valerie drew a small disc recorder from inside her handbag, which had been lying on the table during the entire conversation. She pressed the stop button and then selected a memory block and pressed the "play" button. We heard Gloria Delgado's words once again, *"I would say doubts, rather than suspicions. Firstly, I found out that Timothy had lobbied very hard...."* Valerie pressed the stop button.

"Bang, bang." She said. I raised my eyebrows questioningly. "The smoking gun you've been after for so long."

"Yes, at last we have something that ties Elgin in directly. Its only Gloria's word against his though, about him discussing the contract with Gloria, I mean. He could still deny everything, and a court might well believe him over Gloria."

"Yes, but it may be enough to convince people to start digging. If that's all we achieve, then its a major breakthrough. And there's more circumstantial evidence. We now know that Elgin went out of his way to become involved in the Tan-Kum-Doc project. Other people will remember that, and put two and two together."

"I told Gloria we wouldn't be using this, not just yet. I meant it. I don't want her to end up like Daphne Gibson."

"She'll have to take her chances." Valerie's voice was venomous, and I didn't have to wonder why any more. But I was the writer, and so if I chose not to write this up just yet, she wouldn't be able to do anything about it. I didn't want to force a confrontation though.

"Look, we'll hold off for a couple of weeks, no more. We've got plenty of leads to follow up on yet. I'm sure we can pull this trick with a couple of those other suspicious deals. There's no point in exposing Delgado to danger until its absolutely necessary."

"Ok, I suppose you're right." Valerie sounded far from convinced. "But two weeks, no more, then I'll pass this to the press, even if you won't."

*   *   *

Once in the street outside the restaurant Gloria Delgado rang her office, complaining of feeling ill and saying she wouldn't be returning to work that day. She then rang Timothy Elgin.

"I've got to see you. Timothy." She insisted.

"Look, I really don't think we have much to say to each other any more."

"I think we have. Its about National Hydro. I know what you've been up to."

"Ah, OK. Look, meet me at the Grapes in Shepherds Market in an hour." He rang off.

*   *   *

The meeting was short. Gloria confronted Timothy with her suspicions, reinforced by what the two *reporters* had said to her. Elgin denied everything, of course, suggesting that Gloria was acting out of revenge. He also told her he would ruin her career if she didn't stop spreading malicious gossip. Elgin's reaction convinced Gloria that the reporters had been right. Elgin had used her. He had probably never had any feelings for her. Gloria cut the meeting short, leaving Elgin in the pub.

Gloria walked the few hundred yards to Green Park station. She was fortunate that the station was served by the underground line would take her to Victoria, her connection for her train home.

As the train drew into the station the crowd around her, mainly tourists, surged forward a foot or so. She felt a thump in her back and toppled forward. As she overbalanced and fell over the edge of the platform, her own weight became the instrument of her death, her body half twisted. Her head turned the rest of the way, her voice rising to a shriek as she realised what was happening to her. Her last conscious thought was that she recognised a face in the crowd, on the platform right where she had been standing. Scott

Davis, her brain told her, just before the red front of the underground train struck her body and ended her life.

CHAPTER SEVENTEEN

It is a sad reflection on our times that the tragic death, apparently by suicide, of a woman in the prime of her life doesn't even attract a few words in the press, unless the death is a murder, or occurs in some sort of bizarre circumstances. Therefore we didn't find out about the apparent suicide of Gloria Delgado until three days after it happened. That we found out at all is entirely due to the diligence of PC Nigel King.

Nigel is a British Transport Police officer who had just completed his probationary period with the force. He was assigned to investigate what, at first, appeared to be just another death by suicide. Nigel did all the usual things, mainly taking the names and addresses of witnesses who were more anxious to complete their journeys than they were about the death of this unfortunate woman. However, the observant Nigel noticed that the area of platform where the incident happened was covered by no less than 3 CCTV cameras. Nigel recovered the DVDs from the security operators, and spent quite a lot of time analysing them.

The type of system that was in use at Green Park station divides the TV viewing screen into quarters, so that four separate cameras feeds can be viewed at the same time. The operator can select which four from all of those connected to the system. In the case of Green Park Underground Station this was in excess of 20. The operator can take a closer look at what's happening simply by selecting the appropriate camera and putting the display onto "full screen" mode, while the other cameras continue to record their images. The cameras work by taking take snap shots every couple of seconds, rather than running continuously, which allows a single disc to be used for recording for far longer time spans. Nigel examined the CCTV coverage several times over, just to make sure he hadn't missed anything.

All three of the cameras he had seen down on the platform showed the incident. The furthest one away was of little use. As the train appeared below the camera a woman appeared briefly in the gap between the crowd and the train, and then disappeared from view as she fell headlong towards the track. The second camera was more revealing. The woman was only a few feet from the camera, which looked down on her from above and to her right. The woman was clearly identifiable as she stood waiting for the train. She then appeared to lurch forward, grasping at the air as though she had over balanced rather than deliberately thrown herself forward. The man standing behind her seemed to be reaching out to try to save her from death. The final view was the most revealing however. The camera was mounted in one of the archways that led onto the platform. The woman's head was just visible, framed against the white background of an advertising poster on the far side of the track. Behind her stood the man who had apparently tried to save her. Nigel replayed the recording once more, just to make sure he was right, then he reached for the telephone.

"Hello, Inspector James? Its PC 149 King. I'm assigned to the death at Green Park yesterday. I have something I think you should see."

"I'm quite busy King. Is it really important?"

"Sir, if I'm right then the woman's death was neither a suicide nor an accident. I think you should take a look."

The Inspector reluctantly agreed, and appeared in the CCTV viewing room a few minutes later. PC King took him through the sequence of video recordings, just as he had viewed them himself. He replayed the final one again.

"What do you see in that one, Sir, how do the man's arms move?"

"Well, they sort of pull back, then in the next frame they reach forward. But I can't quite see what you're getting at."

"Bear with me, Sir. Perhaps a demonstration would help. Imagine you're the man in the video, and you see the woman in front of you start to fall forward. Make a grab for her."

The Inspector played his part out. "See, Sir, your arms came up from your side and reached out in one smooth movement. But in the video the man's arms move backwards, from the elbow, first and then forwards and up. Try it."

The Inspector did so. "Why would someone make a move like that, Sir? It doesn't make sense. And If you look sir, the woman is actually stood still, her head hasn't moved from one frame to the next. It doesn't move until the frame afterwards, when the man has actually started to move his arms forward. If he was trying to save her his arms wouldn't move until after she started to fall, unless he was telepathic and knew what she was about to do."

"It does make sense if the man wants to put some power into his movement, to get more impetus, if he wanted to push, rather than grab at the person in front of them. Well done King. I think we have a murder here. I'm afraid that it's out of your hands now though, this is one for CID to look at."

The Transport Police Inspector saw PC King's crestfallen look at this news. "Look, you've made the break through on this, so I'll see if I can get you seconded to the investigation team. I'm not promising anything though."

*   *   *

CID agreed with everything the PC King told them. The death was an apparent murder by the man standing behind Gloria Delgado. An incident room was established at Charing Cross Police Station, and the case was assigned to Detective Inspector Chris Miles, a veteran of a dozen or more murder investigations. After much lobbying from the Transport Police Inspector, PC King was seconded to the investigation.

At the first briefing DI Miles asked for updates on what had already been discovered. A young woman Detective Constable, one of the first to be assigned to the investigation, explained what had already been established, firstly by PC King and then subsequently by herself.

"Mrs Gloria Delgado, on Tuesday 27th she told her assistant that she had a luncheon appointment, and left the office just before midday. Not unusual in itself, but not a common occurrence either. She usually Pte a sandwich at her desk. At around 2.00 pm she rang her office, saying she wasn't feeling too well and was going home. Mrs Delgado commuted daily from her home in Surrey to Victoria Station, then by Circle or District line to Westminster Underground Station. At 3.30 pm she died after falling under a train at Green Park Underground Station. Or rather, it now looks like she was pushed under the train.

Mrs Delgado was married to a lecturer at the University of Surrey at Guildford. She has no children. At the time of her death her husband was lecturing a group of Business Studies students. Although he can't be ruled out as a suspect, perhaps a conspirator, we're doubtful about that line of inquiry.

According to the post mortem results, Mrs Delgado was a fit, healthy woman who died of injuries sustained in her fall in front of the train. Her blood alcohol level was high, about the equivalent of three doubles of something like gin or vodka, enough to make her unfit to drive. While this wouldn't normally have been enough to make her unsteady on her feet, the fact that she hadn't eaten since breakfast time could have made her feel temporarily unstable, maybe a dizzy spell or something like that. If she went out for lunch we have to ask why she hadn't actually eaten since breakfast time.

Mrs Delgado's mobile 'phone was recovered from her handbag, although it was damaged we were able to extract the SIM card, which has now been analysed. We've also contacted the 'phone networks, several of them in fact. Between leaving her office and her death Mrs Delgado made two calls. The first was back to her office, the call where she said she wouldn't be returning. The other was made straight afterwards, to another mobile number. We're trying to find out who the owner of that number is. Obviously it's quite crucial. Both calls were made from somewhere in the around the Wardour Street and Old Compton Street area in Soho. The 'phone company can't be any more precise than that."

"Thanks, Angela, that's a good start. Keep following up on the telephone connections. Now, what we do need to know, as a matter of urgency, is Gloria Delgado's movements from the time she left her office, to the time she died. Where did she go? Who did she see? Who saw her? Who did she speak with? In particular I want to know what she was doing in Soho, then why she re-appears in Green park Station? There are other Victoria Line connections closer than that."

Assignments were handed out, with even Nigel King being given something to do.

*   *   *

The following day's briefing revealed that considerable progress had been made. PC Nigel King was the first to report.

"I've been looking at how Mrs Delgado might have got to Green Park. As you know, Soho is approximately square in shape, with an underground station at each corner: Tottenham Court Road, Oxford Circus, Piccadilly Circus and Leicester Square. If we take the furthest away from Green Park first, which is Tottenham Court Road, the most likely route for Mrs Delgado to take to go home would be the Central Line to Oxford Circus then Victoria Line to Victoria. There would be no reason for her to get off the train at Green Park. Likewise, if she had travelled from Oxford Circus itself. If she had gone to either Piccadilly Circus or Leicester Square she would most likely have taken the Piccadilly Line to Green Park, then changed to the Victoria Line.

Now, the timings. From the time of the 'phone call to her death was roughly 90 minutes. I did the journey from the centre of Soho, via the furthest station, Tottenham Court Road, to Green Park. It took less than 30 minutes, leaving 60 minutes unaccounted for. I've already checked with London Underground Operations; there were no delays on the Central Line, Piccadilly Line or Victoria Line at the times in question. I've viewed CCTV footage of the downward escalators, and the stairs, at all the stations,. She doesn't appear on any of them between 2.00 pm and 3.30 pm. She does however appear on the downward escalator at Green Park at 3.25 pm. The conclusion I have is that however she got to Green Park, it wasn't by underground."

"Good work Nigel." Commented DI Miles. "I'm not sure what that tells us yet, but it does tell us some areas we can ignore for now. Who's next?"

"Me Guv." Angela raised her hand. "Telephones. Very revealing. The second call that Mrs Delgado made was to a 'phone registered in the name of Right Honourable Timothy Elgin MP." Muttering broke out around the room.

"Quiet, please, quiet." Admonished DI Miles. "The fact that she 'phoned an MP may, or may not, be significant. After all, Mrs Delgado was a senior civil servant, who probably spoke to MPs every day. Angela, please carry on."

"OK, well, we followed up on Mr Elgin's own 'phone calls, just as a precaution. He made three calls himself. All from the Mayfair area. His office is in Westminster, and according to his Press Officer that was where he was all day on Tuesday. So we have a mismatch. One of the calls was made to a Government owned mobile, which is carried by Elgin's driver, Bob Watkins. The other two calls, one timed at 2.10, shortly after Mrs Delgado rang him, and the other at 3.07. Both were to a mobile registered to a company called Get Real Communications, which we've established is a PR company based in Hackney. The Managing Director of the company is a man named Scott Davis. Further checks revealed that Mr Davis has a record as long as my arm, and most of his form has an element of violence to it, GBH, ABH, assault, etc. However, its all old stuff, nothing on record for the last 15 years.

The first call Mr Elgin made to Get Real Communications the recipient was in the Wandsworth Common area. The second one the recipient couldn't have been more than a hundred yards away from Mr Elgin.

"The final telephone related evidence," the police officers in the room noted the introduction of the word *evidence* rather than *information*. Is that someone used the Get Real Communications mobile 'phone at 3.35 pm to ring Timothy Elgin. The call was made very close to Green Park Underground Station.

We have Mr Davis's mug shot, but its 15 years old, so we can assume that he has changed a bit since then."

"Excellent work, Angela. OK, Shaun next I think."

Shaun straightened up and picked up a sheaf of papers. "We've been doing some work on the video stills that Nigel here provided for us. They've been digitally enhanced. The picture still isn't good, but we have a face that could be recognisable to someone." Shaun handed out the papers he was holding, which were copies of the enhanced video photograph. "A comparison of the mug shot with the video still isn't anywhere near conclusive. True, it could be Davis, but it could also be a million other people. It certainly isn't clear enough to make an arrest yet.

An interesting thing popped up when we were looking into Mr Scott Davis. His name has been flagged by the Ministry of Defence Police, about four years ago. The flag is still active. We've put in a call to the MOD Plods to see if anyone might recognise Mr Davis."

"OK, good, well done everyone, some good solid police work there. I'm going to go public on this. We need to try to find out where Gloria Delgado spent that missing 90 minutes, so we need to put her photo into the public domain. I'm going to hold a press conference today. I hope to make the later issues of the Evening Standard, and probably the local tea time news. I don't think this would interest the nationals, but you never know if it's a slow news day. I've set up a *hot line*, which I'll need a couple of you to man." He went on to brief them on the tasks he wanted carrying out.

*   *   *

In both the restaurant business and in pubs the flow of customers has peaks and troughs. In restaurants the trough is from mid-afternoon to the early evening, after the lunch time rush and before the start of dinner. In pubs its much the same, but they get an extra peak of traffic as people start to head home from work, and the stressed and the thirsty pop into a convenient hostelry to quench their thirst. During the slack periods, however, when the tidying up and the place settings have been completed, staff have a period of calm when they can sit back and chill out. Some use the time to catch up on the day's events, either by watching TV or reading the evening newspaper. In the Gloria Delgado case this was extremely fortunate for the police.

DC Angela Cross introduced herself to the waiter who had called the hot line. The Maitre D' was far from happy, as the dinner time rush was just starting, but he didn't want to upset the police. He sent the waiter and the policewoman through to the staff rest room.

"Yeah, I recognised the 'photo straight away." The waiter, Tony, said. "Firstly she was a good looking woman, but also when she arrived there seemed to be a bit of a row."

"What was the row about?"

"I don't really know. I wasn't close enough. I showed the lady over to the table, just as I'd been asked to. She didn't recognise the people that were there, and that seemed to surprise her. Anyway, I was on my way back to the front desk when I heard raised voices, just a few words. Anyway, by the time I had turned round it seemed to be over, and the woman went back to the table and sat down. I served them a few drinks, and then she left. After that the two people, a man and a woman, stayed on and had something to eat, and more drinks. They didn't leave until, oh, must have been nearly 4 o'clock."

Angela produced two photographs, and handed them to the waiter. "Do you recognise either of these two people?" she asked.

"Well, this one," he raised the photo he was referring to, "is that MP bloke. Always on the TV, but he's never been in here. The other one I haven't a clue about. Never seen him before."

"What was the name that the table was booked in?"

"I'll have to look that up, the diary's on the front desk."

Just a mile away, in a pub in Shepherds Market, DC Shaun Pollock was having a similar conversation with a young New Zealand barmaid.

*   *   *

The morning briefing was in session. Angela had the floor.

"We've checked on Ron Hutchinson of National Hydro, the name the table was booked in. At 2.00 pm on Tuesday he was in a meeting with several independent witnesses. He's never been to the restaurant in question. The restaurant's security video was no help. It records to a hard drive and records over the old images as it goes, on a 5 day cycle. By the time we got it the recording for the day in question was erased. We have a general description of the man and the woman, but they aren't likely to be of much help. They're in the file if you want to take a look at them."

"Thanks Angela. So not much progress at the restaurant end. A minor argument, followed by a liquid lunch, and then Mrs Delgado left, at 2.00 pm, as we already thought. The people she was with stayed another 2 hours. Unfortunately they paid with cash not credit card, so they have to remain a mystery for the time being, but we can be reasonably sure it wasn't either Timothy Elgin or Scott Davis. Nigel, what have you got for us?"

"I've been checking the Westminster end. We have Timothy Elgin on security video leaving The Houses of Parliament just after 2.00 pm. We've confirmed with Bob Watkins, his driver, that he took him to the Piccadilly entrance to the Burligton Arcade and dropped him there. He picked him up at the same place at about

3.30, after being summoned by 'phone. Watkins tells us that he's dropped Elgin off there loads of times, usually during the day. He suspects Elgin of having a bit on the side, and that he cuts through the arcade and picks up a taxi at the Burlington Gardens end.

Finally we have Mr Elgin on video returning to Parliament at 3.50 pm."

"Thanks, Nigel. So, we know that the Houses of Parliament records aren't accurate, but we can't be sure whether its a deliberate lie or not. Shaun, I think you have the cherry on the cake for us."

"Yes, Guv. According to Maria Easton, barmaid at The Grapes pub in Shepherds Market, Timothy Elgin met Gloria Delgado somewhere around 3.00 pm last Tuesday. She's absolutely sure about both of them. The meeting was short, and they seemed to be arguing, though they kept the noise down. Mrs Delgado left at about 3.10 pm. There's no CCTV coverage I'm afraid. The security cameras are all pointing the wrong way, both inside the pub and outside.

But that's not all. Maria recognised Scott Davis straight away, even from the old photo. He meets Timothy Elgin at the pub quite often. The routine's always the same apparently. Davis arrives, buys a lager for himself and a double scotch. Elgin then arrives and drinks the scotch, while they talk. They're very rarely together for more than a few minutes. On Tuesday last Davis arrived at about 2.30 pm and left no later than 2.45 pm."

"Excellent. Well, I'll be calling on Mr Elgin today, to ask him about those meetings. However, we have one final bit of news to share with you today. Steve?"

'Steve' was the uniformed Sergeant that was managing the incident room for the team.

"Yes, Guv. Well, as you remember, we asked the MOD Plods, sorry, Ministry of Defence Police, what they knew of Scott Davis. They wouldn't say a word, claimed National Security and referred us to Special Branch if we wanted to see anything that they had. But we e-mailed the video still from the underground. They faxed us back a signed statement from an Inspector Jim Marshall. He confirms that the man in the photo is Scott Davis. He can say this with reasonable confidence, having spent some time in Davis's company a few years ago. The circumstances of the contact, however, are classified.

And one other thing, just to close things off. Young Nigel carried out a further review of the video tapes at Green Park. They produced an excellent image of Scott Davis stepping off the escalator just a couple of seconds behind Gloria Delgado. Had she turned and seen him it might just have saved her life."

"Thanks Steve. OK, let me summarise. We have Gloria Delgado having a liquid lunch following a minor argument, in a Soho restaurant with a man and a woman, as yet unidentified. She then appears about an hour later in a pub in Shepherds Market, where she meets Timothy Elgin and has a row with him. Timothy Elgin and Scott Davis were seen together in the same pub just a short while before that meeting. Finally, we have a positive ID of Scott Davis as the man who appears to have pushed Gloria Delgado off the platform at Green Park Underground Station. Finally, we have the three telephone calls between Timothy Elgin and a mobile registered to Get Real Communications, a company headed up by Scott Davis. Any questions? No. Good. Lets get to it. Nigel, stay with me for a moment."

The other officers went back to their work, while Nigel joined the DI.

"Ever met an MP, Nigel?"

"No Sir, never."

"Go and change your uniform for a suit. I think its about time you did. Meet me at the Police post in The Houses of Parliament at 2.00 pm."

CHAPTER EIGHTEEN

Timothy Elgin had been a worried man for several weeks now, but that worry was turning rapidly to pure terror. In a few minutes time two police officers would walk into his office, and he had no doubt at all what they wanted to know. He had watched a local TV news programme, waiting to see coverage of himself opening a new shelter for homeless people. Because of that he had seen, to his horror, a picture of Gloria Delgado, and the lead story of the evening, the hunt for her murderer or murderers. One of the police officers now coming to interview him was the one he had seen describing the circumstances of Gloria's death, and appealing for any witnesses. Davis had been under strict instructions to make things look like an accident, but it would seem that he had bungled it again.

There was a special department within the Metropolitan Police charged with dealing with high profile people, whether they be the victims of crime, witnesses to it or were suspected of having committed criminal acts. It had been that department that had contacted his Diary Secretary and requested an interview. He had played it cool, of course, as though he was more than happy to assist the police in any way he could. They offered him one of their own officers to "assist" with the interview, but he had declined. The department was staffed by people who were all too well acquainted with people like himself, he knew. There was always the chance that he might give something away, something an ordinary copper might just miss.

The police had obviously made a link between Delgado and himself, but what the link was, and how they had made it, was beyond him. Paranoia gnawed at him. Had someone talked about the Tan-Kum-Doc deal? Had someone seen them together? The police would no doubt give nothing away. He had to be ready with his cover story. Best to keep it simple, keep it as close to the truth as possible.

Elgin's intercom buzzed, to announce the arrival of the two police officers. He instructed that they be shown in.

One officer, obviously the senior one, was in his forties, heavily built, one might even say running to fat. He had the world weary air of a man who had seen too many things that no person should ever see. The other was young, fresh faced, hardly out of short trousers to coin a phrase. The DI introduced the two of them, and accepted the chairs that were offered.

Elgin decided to get in first, to establish an atmosphere of innocent curiosity. "Detective Inspector, how can I help you. You said you wanted to interview me in connection with a death, but I can't say that I know what you were referring to."

"Of course, Sir. No reason why such an occurrence would spring to your mind, I'm sure, but we have reason to believe you may have met the victim. Any insight you can provide us with would be helpful." DI King watched his suspect carefully. Elgin was a politician, and lies, halve truths and dissembling were part of a politicians stock in trade. "Let me provide a few details. I'm leading an investigation into the death of a member of the Civil Service, a Mrs Gloria Delgado. My understanding is that she's known to you, and I wondered if you would care to tell us what you know about her."

"Ah, I see, Gloria, of course. I saw the TV news. I'm not sure I can be that much help. Yes, I knew Gloria, but not very well, I'm afraid. We worked together for a few months, oh, about 18 months back it would have been. But it was a purely professional relationship, you understand."

"Of course, Sir, I wouldn't wish to imply anything else." Chris Miles paused and directed a level gaze at Elgin. "And when would you have seen Mrs Delgado last?"

Elgin's heart skipped a beat. Could he get away with the lie? Did they know about Shepherds Market? He took a gamble. "That would be at least 12 months ago. There was a cocktail party, marking the signing of the contracts to build a new dam in South East Asia. That was the project we were both working on, you understand. We were both present, and I would guess that we chatted at sometime during the evening. In fact I'm sure we did. That would be the last time." The young constable made some notes in his notebook.

"Thank you, Mr Elgin. Can I just clarify, then, that you haven't met Mrs Delgado since that day?"

"No, Detective Inspector. I haven't. We work in different areas of Government. We may have been thrown together for a short while, but that was all."

"Thank you, Mr Elgin. Perhaps if I could ask you one or two more questions, just before we leave."

Elgin relaxed. They were about to leave. That had to be good, didn't it? He gave them his second best smile, the one he used for influential constituents. "Of course. I'm, happy to help in any way that I can." The question, when it was asked, hit him like a body blow.

"Where were you between 2.00 pm and 4.00 pm on Tuesday last, Sir? That would be the 27th."

The smile slipped a fraction, but Elgin forced himself to keep it in place. "I was here all afternoon, I'm sure." The constable made another note.

"Ah, That isn't quite what we've been led to believe, Sir. You see we have security video of you leaving this building, and then returning later. We also have information from your driver that he took you to the Burlington Arcade, and picked you up an hour or so after he had dropped you off."

Elgin let out a laugh, not quite hysterical. "The 27th, of course. You're quite right. I'm sorry, I was thinking of the Monday, the 26th. Yes, I did go out on the 27th. I went to my tailor's for a suit fitting."

"And your tailor will be able to confirm that, will he Sir?" DI Miles saw a man on the ropes, and he wasn't about to let him off them.

"Probably not. You see I didn't go in the end. I had a vicious headache, so I just wandered around for an hour or so, trying to get some fresh air."

"Any witnesses to that Sir?"

"Do I need witnesses, Detective Inspector?"

"They would be useful Sir. You see, we have evidence from an eye witness that you were somewhere else. Somewhere quite specific. You wouldn't care to comment on that, would you Sir?"

Elgin saw that he was trapped like a rat. They had done just as he had anticipated, and concealed what they knew, letting him tell lie after lie until he had incriminated himself just by telling those lies. He should have known better. It would have been better for him to admit that he had seen Gloria that day. Now he had no option but to admit to the meeting and hope that he could persuade them that it was all an innocent misunderstanding.

"Ah, yes, I see. Look, Detective Inspector, I'm a very high profile politician. My enemies in politics would like to see me damaged. Just the slightest human failing would be enough for them to pounce on me. Can I rely on your discretion?"

"Sir, I'm investigating a murder, and that's all I'm interested in. If you have, shall we say, committed some small indiscretion then that is of no concern of ours."

"Thank you, Detective Inspector. I appreciate your co-operation in this. I think you may have already worked out that my relationship with Gloria Delgado was a little more than just professional. We had a brief affair. It all ended quite amicably over a year ago. But on that Tuesday she rang me up and asked to meet. She said it was urgent. I agreed, somewhat reluctantly, to meet her. I went to a pub I know in Shepherds Market and we met there.

She told me she had seen the Sunday newspaper articles about my wife, and she sympathised with me. She said she still loved me, and it was the perfect opportunity for us to get back together again. She would leave her husband and move in with me. I had to tell her it wasn't on. Both politically and personally I couldn't be seen to be breaking up her marriage. She wasn't happy, I can tell you, but that's all there was to it. I could see she was quite distraught, but I couldn't console her. She left in tears. Poor woman. I guess she must have killed herself because of my rejection of her."

"Yes," agreed the Detective Inspector. "I could see how that would be. If she had killed herself that is."

"You mean it wasn't suicide?"

"I made it quite clear in the TV appeal, Mr Elgin. I'm looking for a murderer."

"How could you possibly know it was murder?" Elgin sounded scornful.

"I'm not prepared to comment on that, Mr Elgin. But I have absolutely no doubt about it. And from what you've just told me, it would seem that you're the last person to have spoken to her before she died." DI Miles let the veiled accusation hang in the air for a moment.

"What can you tell us about Get Real Communications, Mr Elgin?"

"What, I'm …." Elgin was thrown by the sudden change of tack.

"Get Real Communications, Mr Elgin. You seem to have had some dealings with them."

"Of course I have. I own them. Its all above board, and noted in the Register of Member's Interests. I set the company up about 15 years ago, using money left to me by my father in law. It provided me with an income while I was a County Councillor. I sometimes use them to carry out research for me, you know, what the man in the street really thinks about the Government, that sort of thing."

"And what do you know about your employee, then, Mr Scott Davis?"

"Not a lot. He runs a pretty tight ship. I hardly ever see him these days. I try not involve myself in the day to day running of the company."

"Did you know that Mr Scott has a criminal record, which involves convictions for some pretty violent crimes?

"No, I didn't know that. I took Davis on a recommendation from my Election Agent, who happens to know him. You can check that with her, of course."

"We will, Mr Elgin. And when did you last see Mr Davis?"

This time Elgin saw the elephant trap opening in front of him. "I arranged to meet with him, briefly, on the Tuesday afternoon, the day Gloria died. It wasn't planned, but he rang me with some query or other about the next Board Meeting."

"He rang you? Not the other way around?"

"Oh definitely, he rang me."

"But the telephone records suggest it was the other way round, Mr Elgin. You rang him from your mobile at about 2.05 pm."

"Ah, but he had rung me earlier, on my land line, from a telephone box I think." Elgin panicked. This wasn't going at all the way he wanted it to.

"That would have been routed through the House of Commons switchboard, then?"

"No, on my home line, before I left for work. Then I rang him later in the day to agree the meeting at The Grapes."

"Ah, of course. That clarifies that matter then." Chris Miles made a show of examining his note book for a long moment. "Hmmm, interesting. I've just remembered, Mr Elgin. Special Branch keep quite close tabs on high profile politicians, for security purposes you understand. They tell me you're staying at your club at the moment, not at home."

"Yes, of course I am. But I meant the same thing. The call came to me at my club."

"And therefore would be routed through the switchboard at your club?"

To the Detective Inspector it seemed as though Elgin visibly deflated. "Yes, I suppose so." Elgin could only hope that the switchboard operator had a poor memory.

"OK, Mr Elgin. We'll look into that. Now, could you tell us about the other two conversations you had with Scott Davis that afternoon. One at about 3.10 and the other at about 3.35 pm."

"Look, Detective Inspector, I'm getting a little tired of this ." Elgin exploded. "If you have an accusation to make against me then make it. I had routine business to discuss with Davis, that's all there is to it. What possible concern could that be of yours?"

"Its a little bit delicate, I'm afraid, Sir. I'll have to rely on your discretion now." He looked at his watch, then made a decision. "You see, Sir, Scott Davis is our prime suspect for the murder of Gloria Delgado. Detectives from my team are in the process of arresting Mr Davis right about now. It would appear that he spoke to you just a few moments after he had pushed her in front of a train, and we wondered if what he had to say to you might be in any way connected with the murder?"

Elgin's face fell. He realised, at last, that the game of cat and mouse was over. "I think I'd like my solicitor present before I say any more."

Detective Inspector Miles stood up. Constable King followed suit. "Of course, Mr Elgin. If you would like to come to Charing Cross Police Station tomorrow at 9.00 am, I would be happy to continue this interview in the presence of your solicitor, and under caution. Good Bye Mr Elgin."

"I'm seeing constituents at that time. I'll get my secretary to arrange a time for me to come to the police station." Elgin tried to salvage some of his dignity and authority.

"That wasn't a request, Sir. If you fail to attend at the time I have said then I'll be quite happy to send a couple of PC's to your office to arrest you, if you would prefer to do it that way. I'm sure the Prime Minister would be interested to know why you are being escorted from the Houses of Parliament by uniformed officers." D.I. Miles wasn't about to let this bully off the hook. No doubt a 'phone call to the Home Secretary would pull the rug from under him, as had happened on a previous occasion, but the policeman hoped that Elgin wouldn't want to draw attention to himself in that way. "Until tomorrow, then Sir." The two police officers left the office, almost hearing the sound of Elgin sagging in his expensively upholstered office chair.

PC King followed his superior officer from the room, feeling that he would probably never witness a more proficient interview again in his life. He felt privileged to have been present for it.

*   *   *

Scott Davis lounged in the chair opposite DI Miles and DC Angela Cross. His whole attitude said that he was unconcerned about being under arrest, and that he felt he was pretty much untouchable. Since his arrest he had repeatedly denied knowing anything about anything, or to use his own words, "nuffink about nuffink."

On his return from Parliament the DI had decided to let Davis stew in his own juice for a while. He had to be careful, of course. The PACE clock was ticking, but the CPS had passed their verdict on Scott Davis and the charge sheet was already being typed up, so the interview was just being used to try to fill in some of the gaps. Although Chris Miles wasn't hopeful, it was always possible that Davis might make a confession.

"OK, Scott." Opened the DI, summarising for the tape recorder. "You've been arrested on suspicion of murdering Gloria Delgado, at Green Park Underground Station on 27th June last. You've also been cautioned and offered the services of a solicitor, which you declined." The Di repeated the caution for the benefit of the tape. "Have you anything to say in response to these accusations?"

"It's all bull shit, and you know it. Someone's trying to fit me up. I've never even heard of Gloria Delgado. And call me Mr Davis, if you don't mind."

"OK, *Mr* Davis. Perhaps you would tell me where you were between 2.00 pm and 3.45 pm on the 27th of last month."

"I was at home, watching the tele."

"Any witnesses to that?"

"Yeah, my girlfriend, Tracy, and her brother Gareth."

"OK, Mr Davis. Do you ever use a mobile 'phone, number 07880 555000?"

"Yeah, it belongs to my company. I use it all the time."

"Is this it?" Miles lifted a Nokia handset off the table in front of him. It had been taken from Davis's pocket when he had been arrested.

"Of course it is. I carry it with me everywhere."

"OK, Mr Davis. Can you explain to me, then, how this mobile was used to make a call from Green Park Underground Station at 3.35 pm on the 27th?"

"You're lying. It couldn't have been."

"I'm afraid its not me that's lying. The 'phone company have computerised records that show this 'phone being used at Green Park Underground Station."

Davis crossed his arm and leaned back in his chair. "No Comment."

"OK, Mr Davis. Lets forget the 'phone for a moment. Can you tell us who this is?"

The DI passed across the photo of Davis on the escalator. "For the benefit of the tape I am showing Mr Davis a photograph of a man, taken just before Mrs Delgado was killed."

"'Ere, he looks a bit like me." smiled Davis. "Now I can understand the confusion. You thought that I'm him. Well its not me. I was at 'ome."

"OK Mr Davis. I accept that it could be mistaken identity. How about this then. We have two witnesses that put you in The Grapes public house in Shepherds Market at 2.45 pm on the 27th. How can you explain that, if you were at home? Oh, by the way, one of the witnesses is your boss, Mr Timothy Elgin."

Davis went white with the shock of the revelation. He had expected witnesses, it was always possible that someone had remembered seeing him, but he felt sure that his *mistaken identity* defence would protect him, especially with two witnesses of his own to lie for him. But for Elgin to sell him out, that was unthinkable.

"No …. no comment. I want my brief." He demanded.

"Of course, *Mr* Davis. I'll get someone to ring him straight away. Interview terminated at 6.15 pm." Miles stood up, and Angela Cross pressed the stop button on the tape recorder. Miles treated Davis to a broad grin. "I hope you haven't made any plans for your Summer holidays, Davis. I've a feeling you'll be spending them on remand in the Scrubs."

Miles called a uniformed constable into the room to escort Davis back to his cell.

*   *   *

Since seeing the news item on Gloria Delgado's death I had been in a bit of a decline. No, that's an understatement. I had been mainly drunk, and when I hadn't been drunk I had been sobbing my heart out. I had also been sobbing my heart out while drunk, but you get the picture. I couldn't avoid the blame. As far as I was concerned I had meddled in people's lives, and as a result they had died. First Daphne Gibson and now Gloria Delgado. My own brush with death magnified my depression and feelings of guilt. I started to wish that the thug with the gun had been a better marksman.

I lay on my bed in my new hotel, my clothes filthy and vomit stained, the floor strewn with pages of the book which I had shredded in my anger, guilt and self pity. They lay strewn amongst the heap of empty pizza boxes like flakes of snow decorating strange angular hills. I hadn't allowed the cleaning staff in, nor any of the other hotel staff. I just wanted to be on my own, to wallow in my own guilt. For once I was sober, as I watched the lunch time news with the sound muted.

The familiar face of the anchorman filled the screen, looking serious, as they always do at the start of the news reports. The lead stories are never about the roller skating rabbits or the centenarian skydivers. The pictures that filled the screen made me reach for the remote control to reactivate the sound. The images of Timothy Elgin walking into a police station certainly grabbed my attention.

" ……. Elgin has today been charged with conspiracy to murder Mrs Gloria Delgado, who died when she fell in front of a train last week. More charges are expected to follow." The picture switched from that of Elgin to a still of Delgado. It was the one that had been used on the local TV news, which didn't do her the justice that her good looks deserved.

The report continued, with Elgin's solicitor assuring us that his client was innocent, and was looking forward to going to court to clear his name. The picture cut to the Prime Minister, announcing that Timothy Elgin had resigned from his post as Deputy Prime Minister, so that he could concentrate on managing his defence, and of course the Deputy Prime Minister had the full support and backing of the Prime Minister.

Various reporters and commentators came and went, giving one perspective or another on the case, however, as the whole thing was now sub judice there was very little they could actually say.

Having said that, the news team manged to spin the story out to fill the lion's share of the programme, switching their attention from Elgin the conspirator to Davis the murder suspect. I felt that my photo should have been up there on the screen along side his. The anchorman had just switched to the minor news stories of the day, you know the earthquakes, hurricanes and famines, when my mobile rang. It was Steven Rycroft.

"Well, old son, we did it."

"All we did was kill another woman." I responded angrily. "We're as guilty as Elgin."

"Calm down, Clarke. I know you feel bad about all this, but it really isn't your fault you know, or mine or Valerie's. Elgin is a nasty piece of work, with at least one other death on his hands, and if you believe that Daphne Gibson was murdered, then its two. The man's ruthless, and would probably have killed again if it suited his purpose." I knew that to be true. He had tried to have me killed, of that we were both certain.

But I couldn't agree with his line of argument. We were the ones who had wound Gloria Delgado up. If we hadn't done that she might never have died. We didn't know, yet, what had happened, but somehow Elgin had seen the threat posed by Delgado and had decided that extreme action was required. Had she been followed? Had she contacted Elgin herself? We would have to wait to find out.

"Anyway, now's the time for the Coup de Gras, old son. You and Valerie must go to the police and make statements about what Gloria Delgado told you. Take the tape along with you, and copies of the draft chapters. Hand them all over to the police, then they'll start investigating him. They've scented blood now, and should be only too happy to start following the trail. Then I think we deserve to celebrate. You and Valerie must come up to the cottage and I'll cook dinner." I didn't feel much like celebrating, but Rycroft wouldn't be denied. We made the arrangements before he rang off.

I agreed with Rycroft that we had to make statements, if only so that the police could properly close the investigation. I rang Valerie and we agreed that we would both go along to the police that afternoon. It was necessary that we arrived together, so that the police wouldn't think there was anything suspicious about our involvement. The one problem we would have would be explaining why we hadn't gone to the police earlier.

Valerie had been staying her brother in Nottingham, and could therefore deny having seen the London regional news programmes and the Evening Standard, which were the only media that had covered the original murder story. I decided that I should have a diplomatic illness, which would allow me to claim that I too, hadn't seen any news coverage on the relevant day. It wasn't too far from the truth if you count alcohol poisoning as a sickness. Once I knew that Gloria Delgado was dead I had been very ill indeed, as ill as serial bottles of vodka could make me. My mood had hardly improved, and I think this is something that will haunt me for the rest of my days.

CHAPTER NINETEEN

Elsa Peters couldn't sleep. She lay in bed staring at Timothy Elgin's back, wondering how she could ever have thought him worthy of her affections. Oh, sure, he was out on bail for the moment, but she felt sure he would go to prison, and in doing so it was always possible that he might take her down with him. Despite his powerful position he was a loser, and she should have recognised it earlier.

Elgin had returned to his home at last. Now that he had been charged the press had to leave him alone or risk being found in contempt of court. Elsa had arrived that evening to try to help him sort out the mess that he was in, though that seemed to be a somewhat Herculean task. As usual, they went to bed together, something they did even when Camilla had been in the house.

Elsa had first met Elgin when she had joined the same Sixth Form as him, at the Grammar School that he had attended. Her family had just moved to the area, so she knew few people. Timothy had been nice to her, shown her around the school and generally befriended her. They had first had sex at the Sixth Form Christmas party that same year, and had slept together off and on ever since. At first they had been *an item*, of course, but later she did it just because sex was a good way of controlling Elgin, getting what she wanted out of him.

When Elgin went to Oxford she had gone to a different University, where she had met and then married her husband. She suspected that Morris Peters had found out about her occasional dalliances with Elgin, he may even have suspected that Elgin was the true father of her child (he wasn't, she was reasonably sure). Anyway, Peters had left her and she had made a point of getting back close to Elgin again. That had been her brother's idea, of course. Otto recognised someone who might be useful, and as the price for his financial support for her and her baby, Otto had encouraged Elsa to cultivate Elgin and, in turn, introduce him to Otto.

When Elgin decided to enter politics he had needed someone to act as his election agent, and Elsa Peters seemed to be the right person for the job. He wanted her on this inside pissing out, rather than the other way around. At least she had managed to persuade Elgin that she was the right person, as she lay curled up in his arms after one particularly energetic sex session. They had never looked back from there. Elsa protected Elgin by acting as a go between for him, making sure Elgin's hands were never dirty, that his fingerprints couldn't be found on any of the deals that he got involved in.

Elsa shuddered as an unwanted memory returned. It hadn't just been Elgin that she'd had to sleep with of course. When he married his wife, Camilla, had shown something of an interest in her as well. That's the trouble with virgins in their late twenties. Once the dam breaks they wanted to try everything, and once Camilla had accepted that Elsa was part of Elgin's life, along with a lot of other women, she had wanted to try her out as well. Fortunately it was a short term interest, but it had never been pleasant.

Of course Elsa had kept records. A girl needs an insurance policy, after all. That was a lesson she had learnt the hard way when her husband had left her. At one time she had thought that she might get Elgin to marry her, but she had seen the sense of the political match that had been made for him. Besides, she could sleep with Elgin pretty much whenever she wanted to, and that was when he was vulnerable. Let his wife put up with his insufferable arrogance and high handed ways; she, Elsa, got what she wanted from Elgin anyway.

Now, however, Elsa was re-assessing her position. Perhaps it was time to cash in her insurance policy and find herself a nice beach to sit on for the rest of her life. She swung her legs over the side of the bed and stood upright. She caught sight of herself in the full length mirror. She patted her stomach. Not bad, she thought. Tits still self supporting, bum not starting to sag yet either. Flat belly. Looks still intact. Hair dye and cosmetics took care of the rest. Choose the right beach and she might be able to find herself a Sugar Daddy to provide for her old age. Men were so easy to fool, she had found out years ago.

David Trace had fallen into bed with her at the first chance that he got, and ended up making Otto close to a million as a result, part of which Elsa had shared. Then there was the bloke at the Foreign Office that had set up the deal with the Republic of Voltava. He had been a real sucker. They had offered him two real beauties to sleep with if he had wanted, but he had confided to Elsa that he didn't fancy either of the two tarts, but would love to go to bed with her instead. She hadn't needed to lie back and think of England, merely to lie back and think of the £100,000 that she was going to make out of the deal. If you're going to be a tart then be an expensive one, she had always thought. Davis had got a good clear photo of the guy's face as he had sweated over Elsa, and that was enough to blackmail him with.

Davis, there was another case in point. OK, he was a nasty piece of work, and had left her with more than one bruise, but Elsa could always keep him in line by sleeping with him. They had needed him of course, but now he was expendable. The longer he went away for the better.

Even Otto hadn't been immune to her charms. OK, she hadn't actually slept with him, that would have been too tacky, but she had always managed to twist him round her little finger. Despite his business skills and his total self confidence in the business world, he was useless around women. Elsa, however, found him attractive young companions that he could go to bed with without having to go through all the agonies of courtship. The idea that she paid the girls never entered his head. Obviously he knew that the girls at the parties were all paid to play, but the ones he saw by himself, sometimes fondly imagining that they loved him, were also being paid well to be there.

She had often wondered why she behaved the way she did. Even at an early age she had known that sex was an easy way to get on in the world. There had been a neighbour that had given her money to run about his house naked, and to sit on his knee and put her hand inside his trousers. That had probably been the start of it, way back when she was just 10 years of age. Then she found that just by suggesting to some spotty teenager that he might, just might, get a kiss or a feel, would be enough to get her a new pair of shoes or the latest pop record. By the time she had first gone to bed with Elgin she was already an experienced seductress, which had been why she had managed to corrupt him so easily.

Men, she thought, how they ever came to dominate the world she would never understand. If only women realised what power they wielded men could be consigned to the dust bin of history virtually overnight.

Elsa picked up her pants and stepped into them. How to cash in on her insurance though? That was the hard part. She glanced over to the sleeping Elgin. He had money of course, her efforts had made sure of that, but getting him to part with it could be a problem. How much might he be prepared to fork out? A million? Half a million? Probably not as much as that. While he had assets worth that much it wasn't likely that he kept that much in cash. Time was of the essence. The longer the police were interested in Elgin the more likely it was that they would find out about her involvement in his dealings. That could mean her arrest. No time to allow Elgin to convert assets into cash then, so she had to look elsewhere.

The newspapers. They always paid well for a decent story, and boy was this a decent story. Maybe she should hire herself a publicist, someone in the Max Clifford mould. No, that wouldn't do. She was guilty of crimes and no publicist dare risk getting involved with her. OK, if she had been to prison and was now selling her story, that was different. But to get involved with her now could itself be a criminal offence. No, if she was going to the newspapers she would have to do the deal herself.

She hooked her bra up and pulled her sweater over her head. Elgin rolled over and she saw the glint of his eyes in the dim light. "Where you goin'?" his sleep laden voice rasped.

"Go back to sleep. I've got to get back up to Wroxborough. You're going to need the local party's backing if you want to play the part of the upstanding citizen. I've got to get back there and start massaging egos." The lies slipped easily from her practised tongue. "God, I hope I don't have to screw the Chairman again." She added, for dramatic effect.

"Bye then. Talk to you soon." Elgin rolled over again.

'Bastard,' thought Elsa. 'You don't care who I sleep with as long as it saves your miserable hide. Well, buster, you're just about to get a screwing you won't enjoy. But I certainly will.'

She straightened her clothing and went through to the lounge to collect her hand bag. On the table she caught sight of the papers they had been reading the night before. It was part of that book that was supposed to be being written. That's how she would do it, she decided. She'd speak to that Sam Walker. She'd know who was interested in buying the real story.

*   *   *

Sam Walker sat at her desk with the two reporters that had asked to see her. They had been tipped off that she knew who was writing the book about the MP, and were anxious to talk to the author, or authors. She didn't like the two men. They were the worst sort of tabloid journalists. She could almost hear the leer in the voice of the one she had spoken to over the 'phone. Now she was with them she could see them visualising her topless, or perhaps even naked, spread over three pages of their trashy newspaper. She felt itchy, as though some microscopic creature was crawling across her flesh. But it doesn't do to upset the opposition, and her department head had given it the Ok providing there was a *quid pro quo.*

There was no way Sam was going to reveal her sources to these two down market hacks. Her first loyalty was to her own newspaper which, although it was less prone to publish scandal, was as anxious as any other paper to publish a "scoop" if it could. On such things are circulation wars won. But Sam was a reporter first, and it was always possible that these two cretins might let something slip which she could pass back to Steven Rycroft.

"We know you know who's writing the book." The reporter of the pair said. "Camilla Elgin" again the leer, "told us you were the go between. All we want is an inside track on it. We'll take it from there."

"I'm not sure if my contacts would approve." Its funny, she thought. If these two were from the Telegraph she'd have no hesitation about offering to contact Rycroft for them. Even if they treated her with a modicum of respect she might have helped a little.

"Look, my own paper is interested in this story as well. They have first call, after all I do work for them.?"

"We're always looking for new talent at our place." hinted the hack. "Maybe we could call this story an introduction fee. I'm sure I heard that the editor of the women's page was about to resign." He put an emphasis on the word "women's" that set Sam's teeth on edge. She fought an uncontrollable urge to jab the very sharp point of the heel of her shoe into his instep.

"Tell you what." Responded Sam. "You get me a job offer in writing and I'll talk to your Managing Editor. I'm only willing to negotiate with the organ grinder, not the monkey. If my own Editor comes to me before that though, I'll be talking to him, and negotiating a raise at the same time."

Her telephone rang. She turned to answer it as if the two reporters had already left the room. She nodded absently as the person on the other end spoke to her. She grunted occasionally, then asked the caller to hang on.

"I'm going to have to take this call, so if you two….gentlemen wouldn't mind finding your own way out." She turned back to her desk with an air of finality.

The reporter eased himself off the edge of Sam's desk, where he had been perched, and signalled his partner that they were leaving. "OK, if that's how you want to play, then we'll find the book by ourselves."

Sam removed her hand from the 'phones mouthpiece and concentrated on her caller. "Ok, Mrs Peters, I'm not sure if your story is going to be of much interest to us."

The reporter's ears pricked up. Mrs Peters, eh? He knew that name. He had spoken to a Mrs Peters when he had been trying to track down Camilla Elgin. Could it be the same one? Coincidences do happen, but sometimes they aren't really coincidences. He couldn't hang around to eavesdrop, even though he wanted to, but he knew it wouldn't take long to find Mrs Elsa Peters if he wanted to.

Same was speaking again. "I'm sorry, Mrs Peters, but as far as I know, no paper has ever paid that much for a story, and even if they had, I can't see what you would have to tell us that would be worth that much, I mean, a few tales of deals done in party committee rooms isn't going to sell many extra copies."

"But that isn't what I'm offering, Ms Walker, may I call you Same? I first slept with Timothy Elgin when I was 17 years old and I've slept with him on and off ever since. I even slept with him last night. I've also slept with his wife. I've been at parties where he has taken both class A and class B drugs...." Sam's chin had fallen open as she listened, and she started making frantic notes "and had sex with prostitutes, some of them quite young and one possibly under the age of consent."

Elsa Peters was pretty sure that the last bit was a lie, but by the time it had been disproved it wouldn't matter. "Then there's the money, Sam" she continued. "The Cayman Islands bank account with over £5 million in it, all in Timothy's name and none of taxed.

How do you think he got that sam? It wasn't by being a County Councillor or an MP." Peters paused an took a big breath. "Finally, Sam, Timothy's business activities may have resulted in two deaths. I don't mean the Delgado woman, that's already in the public domain. I mean two others. Now do you think my story is small beer?"

Sam had been doodling next to her notes. She looked at what she had written. First was the price £1,000,000. The second was three large letters. O.M.G.

Sam took a big breath and gave her answer. "Mrs Peters, I'm not qualified to negotiate on this. I'll have to take it to my Editor. But he's going to want something substantial. We only have your word for all this." She didn't add that a traitor's word was never trusted, even by the press.

"Ok. I've got names, dates, places, photos and even some video. What do you need?"

"A photo of Timothy Elgin in a compromising position with a prostitute should be good enough, but make sure its real. We have experts that will spot a photoshop job in a flash."

"I've got a bit of video that should do the trick. I'll get it biked over."

Sam took Elsa Peters' contact details and then hung up, promiosing to get back to her by the end of the day. She almost tripped over her feet as she sprinted to the lift that took her to the editorial floor.

Steven Rycroft met me at Banbury Station, as agreed. He navigated us through the town until we were on the main drag, heading South into the Oxfordshire countryside. We passed the jumble of buildings that made up the Horton Hospital, then Sainsburys, and finally Banbury Rugby Club, and the bulk of the traffic was finally out of the way. As Adderbury appeared on the horizon Steven relaxed a little, and filled me in on the latest developments, particularly Elsa Peters selling her soul to the tabloid journalists.

"Once they've published the story we can get our book out close behind it. We should make a killing. My agent has spoken to your agent, and she's already negotiating film and TV rights. This story is going to be a hot one. If we time it right we can be ready to hit the screen as soon as Elgin is convicted."

We couldn't publish anything factual now that might incriminate Elgin without risking an action for contempt of court. We had considered changing all the names of the characters in the book to their real names, but that wouldn't be possible if we wanted an early publication date. However, I was already working on a TV script, that would hopefully also become a film, and that named names. Filming could start on a closed set, ready for showing on the day when Elgin went to prison.

My mind was still filled with pictures of Gloria Delgado and Daphne Gibson, so I couldn't quite share in Steven's exuberance. I sat in silence, watching the rolling Oxfordshire fields speed past at 50 mph. Rycroft is a very law abiding driver.

"Oh, come on, snap out of it, Clarke." Rycroft tried to cheer me up. "Hey, I've put Valerie in the room next to yours. Play your cards right and you might be on a winner there you know. She quite likes you." I ignored the salacious suggestion. It wasn't Rycroft's style, and he was obviously just trying to raise my spirits, but even the thought of a night of passion with Valerie couldn't help me.

Valerie and I had gone to Charing Cross Police Station as agreed, and had told our story to the police. The female Detective Constable, Angela, had been grateful to be able to tie up the loose end concerning who Gloria Delgado had met in the restaurant. She was extremely interested in the tape recording and the draft chapters of the book, copies of which we provided for her. She was certain that the tape in particular provided a better motive for conspiracy to murder than some vague notion of emotional blackmail. Angela seemed to accept our stories about not having heard about the murder until Timothy Elgin had been arrested. I think the material we gave her distracted her too much to give it more than passing attention. Besides, we were small fry. The big fish were Elgin and Davis.

Valerie had shared a cab home with me, as far as Angel tube station. I had moved back into my flat following Scott Davis's arrest.

"You look like shit." She said, as the cab manoeuvred its way through the central London traffic.

"Thanks." I said. "I feel like shit."

"Steven told me about it, you know, feeling responsible for Gloria's death. It isn't true. You told her to keep a low profile. She obviously didn't. I had a girly chat with that policewoman after I gave my statement. Apparently she left the restaurant then telephoned him straight away, then went and met him. She might as well have put a gun in his hand and invited him to shoot her. Very indiscrete of her, Angela I mean."

Valerie's words didn't make me feel any better. The truth, as far as I was concerned, was that if we hadn't contacted her then she would still be alive. OK, Elgin would still be free and clear, but there were other ways of getting Elgin. His murder of Gloria demonstrated how vulnerable he really was, and how rattled we had made him. OK, that conclusion was reached with the benefit of hindsight, but it should have been apparent to us after Rycroft's house had been trashed, and certainly after the aborted attempt to kidnap me. The problem was that I was working with two people with strong motivations, and they weren't bothered about who got hurt in their pursuit of Elgin. I understood Valerie's motivation now, but that just made Rycroft's more elusive.

Here was a professional TV journalist, very successful and highly respected in his field. I could understand it if he was working on an exposé of Elgin to enhance his own career, up to a point I could anyway. Besides, the best he was going to get out of this, professionally speaking, was a co-author credit. This seemed more personal, more like Valerie's motivation. I ruled out Rycroft being

Valerie's unaccounted for brother; He was at least 20 years too old. Also his accent and antecedents ruled him out of having any connection with Wroxborough. Rycroft was Anglo-Irish. His father had been a British Army officer and his mother a Belfast school teacher. They had travelled the world living in British Army garrisons, before finally settling in rural Yorkshire. The only connection Rycroft seemed to have with Elgin was that they had both gone to Oxford.

The Oxfordhire countryside seemed to grow dim as lights exploded inside my head. Of course. Oxford! Rycroft and Elgin were close enough in age for them to have been at the University at the same time. Had they met? Had they known each other? Had they had some sort of conflict, a falling out? Had they even been lovers? It would have had to have been something big to stir up this level of vindictiveness.

I was staying at the cottage for the weekend, then I was due to return to London by train on Monday morning. Banbury to Oxford by train was a 20 minute journey. Perhaps I could even persuade Steven to drop me in Oxford in preference to Banbury? We would see.

The rest of the journey passed in a blur as I wrestled with the idea of Steven and Elgin having some sort of student feud. Steven had given up trying to cheer me up, and left me to mope as much as I felt necessary. But I wasn't moping anymore; now I was thinking. The car turned off the main road and Steven drove us along a narrow lane, grass growing along the crown of the road like a punk rocker's

Mohican. The lane ended at what had once been a farm, but which Steven now referred to as a cottage. Some cottage.

It was old, for starters, the small, narrow windows spoke of Jacobean architects. It had probably been the property of a wealthy landowner at one time, what we would now call a gentleman farmer. It wasn't quite big enough to call a stately home, but if it had been human it would have had pretentions of grandeur. The out buildings were gone, having been replaced by a modern garage big enough for at least three cars. The house was elegant, solid, and screamed money at you.

Gardens surrounded the house, carefully tended. A gravel drive wound through them to the front door and then to the garage beyond. To the side I could see trees, probably an orchard. No doubt more lawns as well. Steven halted the car directly outside the front door. I only had one small holdall and my laptop, but Steven took them from me anyway, ushering me into the front hall.

I had expected dark wood panelling, but the hall was light and airy. Windows above the door allowed the sunshine to stream in. Sporting prints lined the wall, huntsmen, hounds and foxes forever frozen on paper, the only gesture towards the house's rural history. A solid, highly burnished wooden staircase angled its way around three walls to the upstairs landing. Steven dropped my bags and took me on the guided tour.

"Lounge," he announced, taking me into the room to the left of the hall. It was furnished just as such a room should be. Polished leather chesterfields dominated the room, which was lined with bookcases along one wall. A large stone fireplace formed a centrepiece. In deference to the time of year the fire wasn't lit. Instead a fire screen, decorated with Chinese motifs, stood in front of the empty grate. Expensive looking oil paintings, landscapes mainly, were dotted around the walls. The only thing out of place was the modern TV and hi-fi equipment that formed an essential part of all homes nowadays. Steven led me through a door on the far side of the room.

"Kitchen and dining room combined." The room somewhat exceeded this casual description. One end was a large cooking area, dominated by an Aga. In the centre was a gas fired cooking range, over hung by saucepans and utensils. Cupboards, work tops and the usual selection of white goods worked their way around the remaining wall space.

The dining area would seat at least 10, possibly 12 at a pinch. A large oak dining table took up most of the space, surrounded by a harlequin selection of chairs. You could almost feel the history oozing out of the wood. An antique sideboard filled the wall beneath the windows that ran down, what I worked out to be, the side of the house.

Leaving by a side door we crossed the hall and into the final room of ground floor of the house. This had probably once been the family room, the main room of the house where the extended family of generations of country farmers had sat and whiled away the long winter nights. It ran from the front to the rear of the house, with windows on two sides and a huge French door, a modern addition no doubt, running the width of the rear wall, giving a splendid view across the garden until it joined with the rest of Oxfordshire, filling the space with varied shades of green and brown, until they faded into soft greys and then gently merged with the pale blue of the Summer sky. The view alone must have been worth half a million pounds. To one side I could just see the edge of the trees that I believed formed the orchard, but which were more easily seen through the side windows of the room.

Having recovered my breath after taking in the scenery I surveyed the interior of the room. At the front, and dominating the first third of the room, was a concert grand piano. Gustav's no doubt. The rest of the room was furnished with comfortable looking chairs and sofas, arranged where the occupants could watch the master play, at the same time as sharing the companionship of the rest of the audience. The last piece of furniture in the room, and jarring hideously with the elegance of the rest, was a modern cocktail cabinet. Steven saw my reaction to it.

"I know." he sympathised with me. "But it was Gustav's mother's and he won't be parted with it. Its a pity you won't hear him play, but he's still on tour. Amsterdam tonight." As he explained Gustav's itinerary we left the room. "....then Berlin, Prague, Milan, Paris and finally two nights at the Albert Hall before coming home." He paused in the doorway to look back at the piano with what could only be described as adoration. "We're planning to get married, now that we can." he confided. "I do hope you'll come. We'll finally be going public. "

We climbed the stairs and Steven turned right at the top, into a room that must have been above the lounge, and which was of similar size.

"Your room." He announced. "Bathroom through there," he indicated the far side, "which interconnects with the room I'm putting Valerie in. The lock on the door on your side doesn't work, so time it right and you might walk in on her by accident." He gave me a leer that Sam Walker would have recognised. This was a side of Steven Rycroft that I hadn't suspected. Or was he just being a bit clumsy in his matchmaking?

Steven had picked up my bag on the way past the foot of the stairs and he now placed it on the bed. We walked back along the landing and Steven pushed open another door. "Valerie's room, when she arrives, he said, before moving on towards the stairs. "My room is on the other side of the landing, and an office over in that corner." He pointed towards a door. "Wander round if you want to, make yourself at home. You'll find just about anything you might want to drink in that horrible cabinet in the music room. There's beer and soft drinks in the fridge in the kitchen, of course, and tea and coffee makings in the cupboards. Please, just don't leave wet rings on top of the piano. Gustav does hate it so. Just help yourself, its Liberty Hall here." With that he left the room, and me.

I have never been a good guest. Although everyone always says make yourself at home I never feel comfortable, always feeling that I'm intruding. However, I did fancy a drink, so I went down to the music room and raided the cocktail cabinet. A large vodka and tonic in hand I decided to explore the house a bit more. Where Steven was I didn't know, but he said feel free to wander around, so I did.

I returned upstairs. I took a quick look into the room Steven had said was his. Nothing spectacular, I was disappointed to see. No whips or chains, just pastel shades of bedding and solid pine furniture. I passed on along the short side of the landing to the office, equipped from the same supplier as the house in Fulham, though much smaller. I went in and sat down in front of the computer. Should I or shouldn't I? Make yourself at home, the man had said, and if I was at home I would use my computer. I switched this one on and within a couple of minutes the broadband connection had me hooked up to the internet.

An hour later I heard a car pull up, followed by a woman's voice drifting up the stair as Steven greeted the new arrival. I recognised Valerie's voice. She, no doubt, didn't need the guided tour, but it didn't take her long to track me down to the office.

"All work and no play, as they say." she greeted me.

"I've got time to make up. I haven't done very much since Gloria Delgado died. I haven't been, shall we say, in the mood."

"If that's how you want to describe it. What are you doing?" she came over and leant forward to view the screen. I caught the smell of her perfume. A very light scent that didn't obscure her own warm, fresh smell. I glanced round and found myself looking at a generous amount of cleavage, revealed by a blouse that wasn't fully buttoned. I wasn't used to such sights, not from Valerie. I was used to the professional Valerie, the one that wore long skirts and modest sweaters. Valerie, apparently, was off duty. I dragged my eyes back to the computer screen, trying to forget what Steven had heavily hinted at during our car journey. "Oxford University Alumni Associations" she read over my shoulder. "Looking for anyone in particular?"

"Just contemporaries of Elgin. Seeing if any prominent names crop up." Fortunately I'd just switched away from the page that had shown that Steven Rycroft had been at Christ Church College at the same time as Timothy Elgin.

Valerie placed her hand on my shoulder. Apart from giving me a helping hand over the wall at Trace's house it was the first time she had made any sort of physical contact with me, other than that necessary for passing and receiving objects. "Clarke, Steven and I are very worried about you. You've taken Gloria's death very hard, we can see that. That's why Steven invited you down here. He's hoping that a couple of days in the country might buck you up a little."

"Thanks, I know Steven thinks he's helping, but what I'm suffering from can't be helped with fresh air. I'm hurting deep in my soul, Valerie."

She raised her hand to my cheek. "Poor Clarke. I hate to see you like this. I've grown very fond of you, you know." That took me completely by surprise, and I silently urged her to continue. "You're a nice guy, which is probably why you feel the way you do. Try to relax, enjoy the weekend. If I can help you to relax in any way, I promise I will." If that had been said by most women it would have been loaded with hidden meaning, but coming from Valerie it just sounded sincere. Unfortunately it also sounded like the words of a friend, rather than those of a lover. I thanked her. She left the room, returning a few minutes later with fresh drinks for both of us.

"I shouldn't encourage you to drink, but what the heck. You've worked hard, you deserve a break. Switch the computer off now, and come down stairs with me. Steven has a fantastic collection of films on DVD. Let's see if we can find one to make us laugh, or maybe make us cry."

I did as I was told.

CHAPTER TWENTY

Things were going well, the reporter considered. The Boss had finally agreed to the woman's asking price after she had provided some samples of the sort of things she could reveal about Timothy Elgin. All the bribery and corruption was good, of course, but it had been the parties, complete with video and stills images that had really convinced him. Political scandal was one thing, but sex sold more newspapers. Poor Sam Walker, mused the reporter. She had the biggest scoop of her life land in her lap, then lost it in a bidding war. There was no way The Boss was going to let this slip through his fingers, and certainly not through lack of money. Elgin had said some very nasty things about The Boss in Parliament, where he was protected by Parliamentary privilege. Now it was payback time.

They had lodged Elsa in a hotel while she told the story. Not just any hotel, of course. This woman knew what she wanted and wasn't shy about asking for it. This hotel had more stars than the Ritz and Savoy combined, and prices to match. The suite was costing more per night than the reporter earned in a week, and despite his vulgarity he wasn't cheap.

Elsa was occupying her usual seat where she could appreciate the views across the rolling Berkshire countryside. Scattered around her feet were the various files and boxes that she had retrieved from her lock up storage container. It had started out just as a safe deposit box, but the collection had long ago outgrown such a facility. The wardrobes and drawers in the suite were packed with her clothes. She wouldn't be going home again.

The reporter was watching a video tape that corroborated Elsa's story about Timothy Elgin being into threesomes. That Camilla Elgin enjoyed such pleasures was now firmly in the public domain, but this latest revelation would show Elgin up as the hypocrite that he was. Elsa had, somewhat reluctantly she said, joined in with Elgin and Camilla on three occasions. The third time she had been the instigator, at her own house, where she had managed to conceal the video camera. Wasn't modern technology wonderful?

"I wonder if we can get some stills off this?" the reporter thought out loud. He was enjoying the spectacle. Elsa let him watch, unconcerned that she was being seen by this creep, naked and writhing in the passionate embrace of another woman, while performing an oral sex act with a man. She could live with that. As long as he didn't try to sample the goods himself she would let him have his simple pleasures. Besides, he would see far more than that before he finished documenting the whole story. She hadn't even started to provide the full lowdown on the parties yet. The tape ended and the reporter reluctantly returned his attention to the fully clothed Elsa.

"OK, I think that will do for today. Mind if I borrow the tape?" He didn't wait for a reply. After ejecting the tape from the machine he dropped it into his shoulder bag along with his laptop. "By the way, we're going to press with this on Sunday week. Front page, two inside pages and a 10 page centre spread. Biggest we've ever done, other than that one on the Queen's Diamond Jubilee. I think this is going to sell a lot more papers though." Elsa didn't look at him. She felt that if she saw that look on his face just once more she might just jam his head in the trouser press. He was only a small bloke, she mused. She was pretty sure she could overpower him if necessary. Without turning round she spoke to him.

"I've pulled out the stuff on the Government deals. You might find it worth while to check out this list of names." She handed the reporter a sheet of paper.

"Who are these?"

"Ministers that Timothy either bullied or bribed into co-operating with him, mainly junior, of course, but one or two big names as well. I was the bribe in one case, and there were prostitutes involved as well, both male and female, so you'll get plenty more sex. I've got photos. You better check with your editor that he wants to use the names. Some of these might feel inclined to sue for libel, though they won't have any grounds." He looked at a couple of names and gave a low whistle.

"We've been sued before, we always win more than we lose. We're insured for it, you know. Of course we can't use anything related to the Delgado murder case, not yet anyway, but there's more than enough so far to make the gunpowder plot look like a sparkler in a non-alcoholic cocktail." The reporter wished her goodnight and left the suite.

A woman came into the room from one of the bedrooms and switched on the TV. She was the official *minder*, hired by the newspaper to make sure that (a) Elsa didn't get second thoughts and make a run for it now that she had the money, and (b) no other reporters were entertained so that Elsa could double her money. Elsa didn't like the woman, considering her to have the intelligence of a newt and the charm of a worm, but it was part of the deal.

Elsa picked her papers up from off the floor and tidied them away in their folders. She had no intention of letting the woman see her naked, even in a photograph.

*   *   *

Valerie and I watched Titanic together. Steven had cooked us an excellent meal, and I must admit I did feel better, more relaxed, afterwards. We went into the garden after the meal and watched the sun sink towards the Cotswolds, chatting idly about this and that. Steven excused himself, saying that he was tired. We heard the piano playing for a short while, then silence fell as the evening twilight started to gather.

"He misses Gustav terribly, you know." commented Valerie.

We went inside and put the DVD in the machine, losing ourselves in the unfolding love story and tragedy of Jack and Rose, as they shivered their way through the sinking of the great ship.

Valerie started out sitting at the far end of the leather settee, but as the story unfolded and she went off a couple of times to re-fill our glasses I found that she had got nearer and nearer to me. At last she drew her legs up onto the seat and laid her head on my lap. I risked putting my hand on her shoulder, and when she didn't object I gently stroked her hair for a while. Valerie had let her hair grow a little since I had met her, and now it curled around the back of her neck. Occasionally my fingers would brush against the skin of her neck.

"That's nice." She whispered at one point, "Very soothing."

Her breathing got deeper and more regular and I realised that she had fallen asleep. I didn't want to disturb her, but at the same time I didn't want to spend the rest of the night sat on the sofa watching News 24. I wriggled out from underneath Valerie's head, and replaced my knee with a couple of well stuffed cushions. I switched the light out and tip toed from the room.

I was naked except for my underpants when Valerie walked into my room. I was about to cover up my naked body when I realised that my arms and hands weren't up to the task. Instead I slipped under the duvet.

"You should have woken me." She said, coming fully into the room.

"You seemed so at peace. I didn't like to disturb you."

"I was comfortable, but it was only because I was sleeping on your lap." She started undoing the buttons on her blouse. Already her breasts were pushing the materiel aside as her hands reached the waistband of her jeans.

"Look, do you think this is a good idea?" I said, hoping against hope she wouldn't say no.

"Probably not." She conceded, "but you've had your eye on me since the day we met, and I have to say I've been flattered by

that. There's no point denying it. You were practically drooling ."
She undid the cuff buttons and slipped the blouse from her
shoulders. Her breasts fell free, unrestrained and unsupported by a
bra. "Oh, to hell with it." she said, discarding the blouse and starting
work on her jeans. "Lets live a little. You do want to, don't you?" a
doubtful tone suddenly entering her voice.

"Of course, yes. You've just taken me a little by surprise."

She smiled. "Good. I hate being predictable." Her jeans hit
the floor, leaving her naked but for the tiniest pair of briefs. "Shift
over, let me in there." She found the light switch and plunged the
room into darkness. I felt her cooler skin against mine as she slid
into the bed beside me.

*   *   *

I woke the next morning and immediately felt a familiar
wave of disappointment wash over me. The bed beside me was
empty, and in my experience that meant that my partner of the night
before had felt sufficient disappointment in my performance to feel it
necessary to steal away in the dead of night.

I needn't have worried. Valerie entered the room right on
cue, carrying a breakfast tray. In my experience this was a good sign,
though one I was less familiar with. I struggled into an upright
position, ready to receive the tray. Valerie placed the tray on my lap
then gingerly perched on the edge of the bed.

"Thanks, this is lovely. You didn't have to do this."

"I know that. Call it an impulse. I went downstairs to make myself a cup of tea, and got a bit carried away." I accepted the explanation, even though I knew it wasn't true.

"Look, about last night." I started to say. Valerie placed a finger on my lips to silence me.

"Don't worry, I'm not reading anything into it. I'm OK with one night stands."

"That's not what I meant. I can't help feeling it was part of a reward, for me being a good boy or something." Valerie stayed silent, looking down at her hands as though they were suddenly very interesting. Oh, no. I'd said the wrong thing as usual and now I'd upset her.

"I realise it could look that way." Valerie said at last. "But I'm not like that, honestly. If I hadn't wanted to go to bed with you wild horses wouldn't have dragged me in here. I like you, Clarke. If, after last night, you don't want to do it again, then I understand."

After last night the thought of not doing it again was something I could barely contemplate. "No, no, I really enjoyed it, and I would love to do it again, honestly."

Valerie smiled at me. "Good. That's what a girl wants to hear." She lifted the untouched breakfast off my lap and set it on the floor. Valerie's robe dropped on top of it, the sleeve landing on the butter dish.

*   *   *

Monday saw me in Oxford. Steven hadn't batted an eyelid when I told him I would like to pop into the town to do a bit of shopping on my way home. He dropped me outside The Randolph Hotel, wishing me God Speed. I watched his car slip through the traffic and turn into Walton Street.

I headed straight for the offices of the Oxford Mail. Without any other starting point I thought it the best place to begin. Although the Oxford Mail's files aren't on the internet yet they are computerised, which made my task a very easy one.

My search came up with three references to Steven Rycroft. Two were quite recent, and covered Steven's return to Oxford for speaking engagements at the University, capitalising on his TV reputation. The third was the one that interested me.

The story was dated at the time when Steven would have just entered his final undergraduate year. It was a small piece, barely two paragraphs. It was a report on the suicide of a student by the name of Paul Walsh. Steven was quoted as a friend of the deceased, saying what a sad loss he felt at the death of his friend.

Suicides, especially of young people, often tell a bitter story and instinct told me that whatever lay behind the death of this young man also lay behind Rycroft's desire to see Timothy Elgin destroyed. I walked across town to Christ Church College. A small sign outside informed me that the college was closed to visitors that day. I realised that it was the height of the examination season, and the college would be anxious to preserve an air of calm about the place, which unwanted tourists would be bound to disrupt. Nevertheless, I stepped into the archway formed by the gate house.

I wasn't sure why I was here yet. I wanted to find someone to talk to about Walsh's death, but wasn't sure how to go about it. Colleges, I knew, were hot beds of gossip and someone was bound to know something, but I could hardly go around asking people point blank what they knew about Paul Walsh. Besides, with the college closed to visitors I wouldn't even be granted admission. What happened next confirmed this to me.

A man stepped out from the Porter's Lodge. "Sorry Sir, but we're closed to the public today. Come back again at the weekend." He wore a smart off the peg black suit and a bowler hat, the signature head gear of the college porter.

"I'm sorry. I saw the sign. Its just that I've come a long way. I don't know why I came really." An idea had occurred to me which might just work. "I really only wanted to take a very quick look. A very dear friend of mine died here, many years ago. I just wanted to see if I could feel anything of him."

"I'm sorry to hear that Sir. Always sad when somebody dies." His routine sympathy didn't extend beyond the surface of his words. "What was his name Sir? I might have known him."

"Paul Walsh. He committed suicide."

"Ah, Mr Walsh. Yes I remember him, and how he died."

"Do you? Perhaps you could tell me about it. I've read the newspaper item of course, but that really doesn't tell me very much."

"I'm sorry, Sir. We aren't supposed to discuss College Business with strangers."

"Well, its my business too you know. He was my ... *friend*." I made a guess that if Walsh was Steven Rycroft's friend then he may well have been gay. I made it sound as though the term friend was a euphemism for my own relationship with the young Mr Walsh.

I had struck a chord. I could see that. "Come with me Sir." He led me back to the edge of St Aldate's. "See that café along there?" He pointed along the road towards the City Centre. On the far side of the road was a small café. I nodded. "Go in there and order a pot of tea. Oh, and some cake. Nothing with nuts in though, they play havoc with my teeth. I'll be along in a few minutes."

I did as I was told. It was a homely sort of place, the café, and the cakes were advertised as home made. The slice I had certainly tasted delicious, and stirred memories of teas at the homes of various elderly relatives. I was munching on a slice of Dundee cake when the porter arrived. He poured himself tea and then set about the slice of chocolate sponge that I had provided for him.

"A bad business, that Mr Walsh dying like that. I think it was bound to happen though, the sort of life he led." He chewed on his slice of cake. I asked the obvious question.

"Drugs. He got himself into drugs. Silly young man. Its not uncommon nowadays of course, but they wasn't quite so popular then. When you get lots of young people you're bound to get drugs, but not many get really hooked, you understand. Most just play at it.

Not Mr Walsh though, he really got in deep. Started dealing on his own account, and when that didn't pay for his habit he started working as a male prostitute, you know, for gay men. Here in Oxford during the week, then up in London at the weekend."

"Was that why he committed suicide?"

"Yes and no. If he hadn't been doing that he couldn't have been blackmailed, so that's the yes part. But it was the blackmail that made him do it, I'm sure of it."

"Blackmail?"

"Well, yes. You can't behave like Mr Walsh did and not have someone finding out about it. The word is that someone did find out and then blackmailed him."

"Any idea who?"

"Only rumours, Sir. Its a big college, could have been a member of staff, you know a cleaner or a gardener, but Mr Rycroft always swore it was a student. If the college authorities had known what Mr Walsh was up to he would have been *sent down* straight away. Big disgrace for him, and for his family as well I suppose. Course, none of this was known at the time. It all came out later. There was a lot of gossip after the suicide, both among the students and the staff, even among the Dons I would guess, though I don't know it for a fact."

"Mr Rycroft? Who was he?"

"He was Mr Walsh's .... *friend* as well. They were inseparable for their first year here. Then Mr Walsh's drug habit got in the way, I think, but Mr Rycroft still looked out for him, made sure he didn't get into bother, got him to bed when he wasn't fit to do it himself. He kicked up quite a stink when Mr Walsh died. Really had a go at the police for not investigating the possibility of blackmail. The Master had to have him in and warn him to calm down. He was creating a scandal, and Oxford colleges don't like scandals. Well, I'm sorry, but I can't sit here gassing all day. Things to do, people to see, as they say." He got up to leave. I thanked him for his help and proffered a £20 note. It disappeared with the practised ease of a conjurer palming a coin.

I sat for a few minutes, finishing off the pot of tea and dabbing at the crumbs on my plate and licking them off my finger tips. Could that be the answer? Was Timothy Elgin the person who blackmailed Paul Walsh? Was that why Walsh committed suicide? It seemed as likely an explanation as any. Faced with a drug problem he was having to prostitute himself to pay for, and the financial demands placed on him by blackmail, he would have been in despair. It could have tipped him over the edge into suicide. Had he confided in Rycroft before he died? That would explain Rycroft's reaction to Walsh's death, and if Elgin was prime suspect as blackmailer it would be enough to explain why Rycroft was so determined to bring Elgin down now. Revenge, as they say, is a dish best served cold.

Of course it might not have been blackmail for financial gain. Walsh was sleeping with men, and some of those men might not have been publicly gay. Knowing who they were would provide considerable leverage. Yes, that was as likely as anything. It would also account for why the police weren't interested. There would have been no money trail to follow, and therefore no proof of a crime.

Satisfied with my morning's work I picked up my grip and my laptop bag and left the café, heading for the railway station.

*   *   *

It was a week later when Steven Rycroft burst into the office. His house in London had been cleaned up, decorated, re-furnished and re-equipped, and Valerie and I were in the office going over the final plan for the book. Up to this point I had been writing pretty much to order, to meet the needs of the campaign against Timothy Elgin. Now we had to take a more structured approach in order to get the book to market in time to cash in on the publicity that would surround Elgin's trial. The fact that a jury still had to find him guilty was, to us, a minor formality.

"Have you seen the news?" Steven cried. He didn't wait for us to answer, but started ticking off points on his fingers. "Practically the whole Government front bench has resigned as a result of yesterday's newspaper story. Timothy Elgin has been arrested again and is being questioned in connection with 'wide scale allegations of bribery and corruption'. Four former District councillors and two County councillors are being questioned. David Trace has walked into Wroxborough Police Station and made a voluntary statement. Finally, the big one: The PM's going to Buckingham Palace this afternoon to request the dissolution of Parliament. A General Election, no less. The opposition have tabled a motion of no confidence and he's getting in first. How does it feel to have brought down a Government?"

I could see that for Steven it was a feeling of great joy. Valerie too looked quite happy. For my own part I wasn't sure. I had never expected this. I had joined up with Steven and Valerie to produce a work of fiction that might, just, lead to the downfall of a corrupt politician, but this was way bigger than that. I thought of the human misery that might go along with this outcome. A snap general election would certainly unsettle The City, and that could lead to job losses and all the grief that went with them. There were the families of all those politicians to consider, and some heads might roll in the Civil Service as well, so what of their families? Then there were the corrupt businesses. How many of them would go to the wall. I wasn't concerned with the shareholders or the senior management, they always ended up in clover, but the employees hadn't done anything wrong, and they would be the ones to suffer most.

"You've got that look, Clarke." Steven observed. "like you just stood in something nasty."

"That about sums it up Steven." I explained my concerns to him.

"Hey, shit happens. If they didn't want to get their fingers burnt they shouldn't have played with fire. Metro want me to front a special on corruption in Government. I've got to get over there straight away. See you all later." With that he vanished from the office.

Valerie turned to me, concerned about my mood. "Steven's right. These people knew what they were doing was wrong. Now its rebounded on them it can't be your fault. And as for the rest, the fall-out, you can't hold yourself to blame for that either. If it hadn't been us then it would have been someone else. You know how journalists are always sniffing around looking for scandals. Someone would have picked something up eventually, and once they did that they would have found their way along the same trail as us."

"Its different for you and Steven though. You had a real reason to do this. I'm just doing it for money. That makes me no different from Elgin, or Elsa Peters or Daphne Gibson even."

"Oh yes it does, Clarke. You haven't done anything wrong. You've just used your talent to follow up a good story and write it in a way that will make people want to read it. You're very different. Anyway, what do you mean, about me and Steven having a reason."

"I know about your father, Vic Ellis. And I know about Steven's friend, Paul Walsh."

"Ah, yes. Well, we always knew you're a good researcher. I shouldn't be surprised about you finding all that out."

"I don't know who your man on the inside is though. I assume it is a man."

"It is. There's no harm in you knowing now I suppose. The chauffeur, the one in Wroxborough. Its my brother Charlie."

"Of course. Billy!"

"No, Charlie."

"Sorry, I meant Billy Allerdice. He said he'd seen Charlie recently, looking quite prosperous. He must have seen him driving the limo and thought he owned it."

"That would be right. Charlie works for the hire company that provided the car for Elgin whenever he was in Wroxborough. He always volunteered for the job. The other drivers didn't mind, because Elgin is such a lousy tipper. Whenever Elgin or his wife were in town Charlie would keep an eye on them. That's how I knew about the pool party. Charlie 'phoned me as soon as he had dropped Elgin off at it."

I wracked my memory. "Surely the drivers name is Knight?"

Valerie smiled. "My name is Ellis, but I call myself Mayfield, my mother's maiden name. The sister we went to live with, her married name was Knight, so Charlie called himself that. We didn't want Elgin, Peters or Davis recognising our real family name. It might have rung the wrong sort of bells."

"And the pictures of Camilla Elgin in the Sunday papers? Charlie?"

"Absolutely. We weren't too happy about that. Charlie did it on his own initiative. We think he may have been getting a bit impatient. He also tipped the press off about Camilla Elgin being in Tunisia. Anyway, it didn't do any harm, and I think it might well have encouraged Elgin to panic a bit more, and trigger off a lot of other things. So you see, Charlie is probably a lot more responsible for Gloria Delgado's death than you are."

"I'm still not so sure. I still feel responsible for that, and I think I always will." The 'phone rang and Valerie answered it.

"More good news. Steven just heard on the car radio that Elsa Peters has been arrested at Heathrow Airport. She had airline tickets for South Africa. That just about wraps up the whole gang. I reckon she'll turn Queen's evidence to save her own skin. After all, she's already sold her story to the papers, so she has nothing to lose."

"How did you and Steven get together?" I asked. I wanted to tie up my own loose ends.

"You aren't the only one who can do research." Retorted Valerie, but with a smile. "When I came to London I needed two things. The first was a job. The second was an ally. I knew I couldn't go after Elgin on my own. I wouldn't have the resources or the know-how. I did pretty much the same as you. I went back to Elgin's early days, in particular his time at Oxford. I cross referred the names against local news stories and came up with Paul Walsh's suicide and Steven Rycroft. Although Elgin wasn't mentioned in any news article its wasn't difficult to find out that he had attended Christ Church at the same time as Walsh.

I did some sniffing around, I was still young enough to pass as a student, well almost. I found plenty of people who knew things, and so I gradually put together the story. I wrote to Steven, at Metro, explaining how we had so much in common, and asking to meet him. I was a bit surprised when he agreed. I'm not sure I expected that. As it happened Steven really did need a PA, so he took me on, and we cooked this up between us. The rest you know of course. You were a later addition to the plan, when we realised that neither of us were much good at writing fiction.

Look, I know you sometimes feel we've used you, but we didn't mean any harm by it. I really am very fond of you, you know. I wouldn't want this to come between us."

"Don't worry." I leaned over and gave Valerie a kiss on her lips. "Just promise me one thing; once we've put this book to bed I never have to hear Timothy Elgin's name again."

Valerie kissed me back, then dragged me downwards towards the floor, where we did something quite unprofessional.

*   *   *

Even after I had moved back into my flat, after I got back from Oxford I hadn't spent much time there. I had stayed at Valerie's tiny bed-sit one night, and then a second, and then a third. Then I'd slept on Steven's couch after a late night of work and wine. Valerie and I were just back from a weekend on the South coast, where we had sat in bed on Sunday morning reading Elsa Peters' revelations in the papers. However, I had to return to my place eventually, if only to do my laundry.

I was tired, and not really paying attention to what I was doing. I swung the front door closed behind me, but the lock is a bit sticky and it bounced open again. I collapsed into an armchair and used the remote control to switch on the TV. Flicking through the channels I found the Channel 4 News, which was recounting the day's events.

I didn't hear anything behind me, so I nearly jumped through the roof when I felt a weight on my shoulder. I looked round to find myself staring into the face of my cat, who had wandered through the open front door. The cat nuzzled my face for a moment, then walked onto my chest and down onto my lap. It curled up, and in a few moments was sound asleep. I picked up the remote control and flicked over to a re-run of Top Gear. Ten minutes later my snoring joined that of the cat's. When I woke up I found Valerie staring at me with a mildly amused look on her face and a suitcase in her hand.

"Seeing as you won't ask me to move in, I'll ask you." She said. The cat slid to the floor and started to wind itself round Valerie's legs.

"The cat makes the decisions in this house, and its seems that you can stay." I replied. I stood up and took Valerie in my arms. I pulled her towards the bedroom and managed to get the door closed before the cat could get in.

The cat sat outside the bedroom door, listening to the sound of clothing sliding to the floor. Realising it wasn't going to get fed it headed out through the front door and scratched outside of Lilly's apartment. The door opened and Lilly looked down at the cat.

"You'd better come in." She said. The cat headed straight into the kitchen and sat, looking expectant. Lilly noticed the door to Nevis's flat was open and went across to shut it. She thought she heard a woman's voice making sounds of passion, but dismissed it. What a strange idea, Lilly thought, Mr Nevis having a girlfriend.

The End

And Now

The author Robert Cubitt hopes that you have enjoyed reading this story.

Find Robert Cubitt on Facebook at https://www.facebook.com/robertocubitt and 'like' his page; follow him on Twitter @robert_cubitt and visit Robert's website http://robertcubitt.com where you can read his weekly blog and learn more about his other books.

Please tell people about this eBook, write a review on Amazon or mention it on your favourite social networking sites

Made in the USA
Charleston, SC
24 November 2015